The Tied-Down Holster

Men disappear around Blue Mesa, New Mexico.

Dick Young, apparently an easy-going artist, vanishes close to a deep chasm in this locality ruled by powerful rancher Walt Guisewell who sees the land he has tamed as his 'kingdom'.

Bob Young, brother of the missing man, arrives and proves very different from Dick. Sometime soldier, sometime convict and sometime lawman, he wears the holster of his Colt revolver tied down by a rawhide thong – the mark of a gunfighter with a reputation and not one to be trifled with.

Looking for answers to his brother's disappearance, he finds that others have disappeared and is soon head-to-head in a bullet-bitten conflict with rancher Guisewell and his crew.

The Tied-Down Holster

Hugh Martin

A Black Horse Western
ROBERT HALE

ISBN 978-0-7198-2017-5

The Crowood Press
The Stable Block
Crowood Lane
Ramsbury
Marlborough
Wiltshire SN8 2HR

www.crowood.com

Robert Hale is an imprint
of The Crowood Press

Typeset by Catherine Williams, Knebworth

Printed and bound in Great Britain by
CPI Antony Rowe, Chippenham and Eastbourne

CHAPTER ONE

AMBUSH AT THE CHASM

Dick Young felt he was being watched as soon as he approached Crouching Lion.

He had the eerie sensation of being under malevolent eyes from the minute he rode up the trail, which was flanked on one side by a long, yawning and deep chasm in the earth. It had once been a course for that luxury here in New Mexico: water.

On the other side of the trail was a sheer rock wall, with a straggling line of tumbled boulders at its base. Some distance from where the boulders ended was the dark opening of a cave in the rock wall. The most significant feature of this trail, carved out of an arid desert landscape, was a rearing bulk of rock at the edge of the chasm.

Looking as if it had been worked on by a master sculptor, it had been carved by aeons of wind and storms into a remarkable piece of statuary resembling a crouching mountain lion, looking down into the deeps of the chasm. So natural was its appearance that it looked as though it might be ready to spring into the chasm in chase of prey.

Dick Young rode under its shadow and his artist's eye took in with admiration the precise touch of genius with which nature had finished the masterpiece.

But the uncomfortable feeling of being watched overrode his admiration of the artistry. He simply knew that he was in a foreboding and dangerous place. Were the unseen eyes those of Apaches, who had the reputation of watching settlers and travellers while, with a secret skill, keeping themselves virtually invisible – until they struck? He quickly dismissed that notion. The Apache had suffered the fate of the majority of Indians at this late stage of Western frontier history. They were long ago tamed, rounded up and confined to reservations.

But the feeling of being under watching eyes persisted.

Dick Young had a sharp turn of mind, given to looking out for the minutest scrap of evidence that might lead to his discovering the reason why two men had disappeared in this location. They had vanished after leaving the nearby town of Sandy Crossing, riding on horses hired from a livery stable.

He was a professional investigator, a fact unknown to the people of the ugly and uncomfortable town to the south, Blue Mesa, which he had made his headquarters.

In Blue Mesa he was known only as an artist interested in sketching the natural features of this harsh land of New Mexico: the rock formations, the wind-sculpted curiosities of the desert, the rocky ridges and the clumps of saguaro cactus. To the hard-bitten men of the sweltering drylands he was a mildly eccentric but harmless visitor. He was not known to carry weaponry, but under his shirt he wore a shoulder harness with a loaded Colt .44 in its holster, and behind his bland facial expression there was an alert mind and an intelligence that had served the military purposes of the Union Army well during the late Civil War.

It was not by mere chance that Dick Young had settled on Blue Mesa as his base. The town had been built up by a powerful rancher, Walt Guisewell, who had tamed this corner of New Mexico and created a large cattle spread. He saw himself as king of the desert-edge cattle ranges and the town of Blue Mesa.

Information had come to the agency that employed Dick Young in Denver, Colorado, suggesting that Guisewell might have some involvement in the disappearance of the two riders. The agency was instructed by the employers of the two men to send an investigator to New Mexico to ferret out the reason for their disappearance.

Part of the brief accepted by the detective agency was the unusual stipulation that what the men were and what they were sent to New Mexico to achieve would not be revealed, even to the detective agency accepting the commission.

Dick Young therefore felt that he was under conditions that handicapped him from the start. He was pursuing the fate of a pair of phantoms who had followed some phantom plan.

He had operated in Blue Mesa as a visitor from the civilized regions who was bemused by the West, still designated 'wild', and its sights and characters. He visited the town's only saloon, the Lucky Dollar and even played cards with hands from Walt Guiswell's W Bar G spread, about whose owner he had suspicions. He kept his eyes and ears open.

He had arrived at this spot called Crouching Lion: the last known whereabouts of the missing men. With his senses alert he rode the trail, feeling the gaze of watching eyes and with his own eyes searching the landscape for any suggestion of a clue to the riddle of the missing men.

He saw what looked like a tiny sliver of paper on the trail in the path of his horse, not far from the jumble of rocks strewn along the trail to his left. He halted his mount and came down from the saddle to pick up what proved to be a small cigarette butt, a fragment of the kind of smoke created by the 'makings', the ingredients of the hand-rolled cigarettes common among riders of the cattle ranges. It appeared to be of very recent origin. Had it been there for any length of time, it would be dried-out and weather-punished.

So, someone had been smoking in the locality. That was not a hugely significant fact in itself, for this trail was used by many people travelling between the towns of Blue Mesa and Sandy Crossing. He wondered, however, if the butt indicated that someone had been concealed in the jumble of boulders strung along the side of the trail, some of which were quite large.

He rode on until he reached a point opposite to where the dark cave opened in the rock wall.

A tract of land slanted up from the trail directly towards the cave. Young's attention was caught by some markings in the surface of this portion of land, suggesting that something heavy had been dragged up it to the cave. He halted his horse and considered the markings, rubbing his chin thoughtfully.

At that moment a rifle blast barked from the cluster of boulders behind him. He was hit in the back and sent jerking forward in the saddle. He twisted his body to look behind him while fumbling with shaking fingers in a futile attempt to get at the weapon in his concealed shoulder holster.

Another blast of firing came, then a third, and Dick Young's last mortal sight was a swimming view of a number of heads crowned by sombreros, looking over the boulders. One face in particular registered on his rapidly fading consciousness. It was that of a glowering man with a distinctive big ginger moustache.

As he slithered sideways out of the saddle he realized belatedly that he had been a fool. He had dismissed the significance of the cigarette butt too easily. There had been bushwhackers waiting in the rocks and he had ridden past them, full into a murder trap, like one who was half-asleep.

His body remained leaning over in the saddle. The murderers emerged from the rocks, six of them carrying weapons, the solidly built man with the red moustache in the lead.

They tramped up to the dead man and his mount. The horse stood pawing the ground nervously, seeming to be aware of the drama of these moments

'All right, you know what needs to be done,' growled the man with the red moustache. 'Get to it quick before someone happens along this trail.'

A pair of his companions lifted the corpse from the saddle while others stripped the animal of its leathers, working with almost savage speed.

'Pete, do we have to deal with the horse, like before?' ventured one of the men. 'Can't we just—'

'No!' cut in ginger moustache angrily. "We already settled all of this. We can't throw a cayuse into the chasm. There are too many rocks sticking out of the sides. You can't throw a horse clear of them to reach the bottom. The whole thing must be dealt with just as we dealt with the other two guys. Now, get at it, damn you!'

The men went at it, sweating, while the bulky man barked orders. He looked towards those who were working on the horse and saw that they had removed the animal's saddle and trappings. To another man, standing by with a Winchester carbine, he nodded. The man stepped up to the horse and the report of his carbine told of the dispatch of the animal.

The men who had stripped the horse began the laborious business of pushing its carcass up the slope of land to the cave. Two more took the corpse of Dick Young towards the lip of the chasm, one holding his shoulders and the other his feet.

They swung the dead man three or four times to achieve the momentum needed to fling him high over the centre of the great gap in the earth. He dropped like a rag doll, to fall to the bottom of the old water course cleanly without being caught on the jagged rocks protruding from its sides. The men nodded to each other, expressing satisfaction. It was a chore of which they had gained expertise.

The saddle and leathers were dealt with in similar fashion, then the two men joined those pushing the dead horse to give some help.

When the scene was wholly cleared of all evidence of the third murderous attack enacted there, he of the ginger moustache blew out his cheeks in relief and drew a palm across his sweating brow.

'Good, let's get back to where we left our horses,' he breathed. He was referring to the little side gully off the main trail, watered by a meagre stream, where horses could be safely left. With a grunt of satisfaction, he added,

'A good thing we managed to get through the whole thing without any interference or being seen!'

He was quite wrong. The act of murder and what followed it had been witnessed from start to finish by eyes well trained in acute observation.

They were Indian eyes – Apache eyes. The Apache people, ancient denizens of the sun-punished desert lands, had a way of keeping watch while remaining virtually invisible to the watched.

CHAPTER TWO

BOB YOUNG COMES TO TOWN

The place seemed to be held by a tangible tension.

It hit Bob Young the moment he walked in. It sang in his ears and gripped his innards. It showed in the eyes of the men standing at the bar, a half-dozen of them, all of whom turned to glower at him as he entered.

They had sly and belligerent eyes set in sun-blackened faces embellished by coarse beards and moustaches and the features of all of them were shaded by the broad brims of sombreros.

Maybe this bunch knew straight off who he was. He had often been told he and his late brother, Dick, were so alike they could be twins.

He stepped with ringing spurs out of the shaft of sunlight let in by the batwing doors. The ugly, dusty sprawl of the street he had just left behind had a sinister, brooding atmosphere, suggesting it was waiting for something dire to happen there at any minute. Such an atmosphere seemed to be the keynote of this whole town, Blue Mesa, New Mexico, nestling close to the border with old Mexico.

That ominous note was echoed with marked intensity in this establishment whose split character was part American saloon and part Mexican cantina. Young entered it five minutes after riding into town with his eyes alert for its sign: *Lucky Dollar.*

He smiled wryly, thinking its run-down exterior signalled hard luck rather than luck of the better kind.

This was the place Dick had mentioned in his letters. Now, Dick had totally vanished and Bob Young had the saloon in his sights as the place to ask questions that might lead to clues as to what had happened to his brother.

He took in the quality of the bunch of men at the bar. They looked to be unsavoury individuals who, as a whole, could make a dangerous package.

He knew that they were taking his measure, too, noting that he was no longer young, that he had a hard-bitten face, a scarred right cheek, grey hair at his temples, lines of bleak experience around his mouth, and alert eyes that were unlikely to miss a trick.

He saw that, in particular, his Colt .45, riding low on his right thigh with the holster tied down with a rawhide thong, took their attention. It was the mark of a gunfighter.

If they believed that his resemblance to Dick meant he had the same deceptive, easy-going and light-hearted style of his brother, his fashion of wearing his gun would disillusion them.

He reached the bar and gave a curt nod to the half-dozen men.

'Hot weather,' he commented.

'Yeah,' growled one of them. 'Damned hot weather.'

The bar was tended by a skinny, bald-headed man who seemed to be intimidated by the collection of hardcases on the other side of the woodwork.

'A beer,' Young ordered without taking his eyes off the men lined up against the bar.

'Sure thing,' the bartender said. There was a weighty lull in which a buzzing fly made the only sound, then a schooner of beer was planted on the bar in front of the newcomer. Young took a gulp of it before tossing coins in payment on the bar. He found New Mexico's oppressive heat so dried up a man that he felt he could drink a river. One of the group raised a question.

'Is your name Young?'

Young turned his gaze on the questioner. He was one of the group whom he had noticed particularly. He was big and solidly built with hooded eyes and a heavy ginger moustache sprouting on a pugnacious face. Young responded slowly:

'I figure you read my brand – the family resemblance. No doubt you'll recollect my brother, Dick, who disappeared outside of town. I wonder if you fellows ever heard it claimed he could have been bushwhacked and that his body was dumped but never found.'

This caused a movement from a squat, paunchy man with a straggly moustache who stood at the end of the line of men. This movement caused Young, whose eyes seemed like those of a predatory beast constantly watching for prey, to switch his gaze to the man. At the same time his hovering right hand dropped in a swift action to grip the butt of his Colt.

The squat man had likewise grasped the butt of his holstered revolver the moment Young mentioned the fate of his brother. For an instant his grip froze in apparent inde-cision, then quickly he loosened his hold on the weapon as Young stared at him fixedly.

The moment the man had moved for his weapon Young received a message flashing through his mind with the speed of a telegraph: *this man knew something about the disap-pearance of his brother.*

The squat man fully understood the meaning of the challenging glint in the newcomer's gaze. Young was daring him to clear leather and attempt to shoot. But the man's mouth twitched nervously and he backed down, allowing his hand to fall to his side, empty.

Young registered his face for the future. He would remember the man with the paunch and how the first mention of Dick's disappearance had immediately spurred him towards chancing gunplay. He was the impetuous type, who would bear watching.

All the men at the bar showed that they felt a chilling moment of tension as this brief interlude was played out, but he of the ginger moustache made an effort to ride over it by carrying on his conversation with Young with as much aplomb as if the incident had never happened.

'I remember your brother. It was too bad about what-ever it was that happened to him.'

'I guess you would remember him. I reckon the whole town would remember him. He was a personable fellow,' responded Young. 'Unless, of course, a lone man vanish-ing right on your doorstep is so commonplace hereabouts that the folks of the town took little heed of it.' He ceased fixing the thwarted gunman with his gaze. The big man scowled.

'Well, it surely shocked the town. Who can say who was

responsible for such a thing? Any ruffian could have killed him, robbed him, then disposed of his body. There are so many drifters and plumb no-account gents lurking this close to the border anything could happen to an unsuspecting stranger.'

'I already noted that,' said Young pointedly as his gaze swept the whole unprepossessing assembly.

The big man had no answer to this observation. He felt he was walking on eggs because while Young held his glass in his left hand, his right one kept hoveriing over – almost touching – the butt of his holstered Colt. As he drank, he looked over the rim of his glass, keeping the red-moustached man under close watch.

The man's companions kept their eyes fixed on Young and his right hand; he was well aware that, with his demeanour and his evident six-shooter savvy, he had brought his own brand of tension into the drinking den. Then the big man spoke again:

'We all remember your brother. He came in here a few times. I reckon he was an all-right sort of gent. He was living a right unusual life as a wandering artist, moving around, sketching landscapes and rock formations and all. He showed us some of his sketches once. All darned good. Are you in the same line?'

'No,' said Young with a slight smile. 'I reckon my skills lie elsewhere.'

It was a pregnant remark; its veiled meaning was not lost on the big man or his attentive companions.

'Of course, we didn't see a whole lot of your brother,' said the big man defensively. 'We don't get into town very often. Too much work on hand at the ranch. My name's Pete Hazen. I'm foreman for Mr Guisewell of the W Bar G outfit. All these boys ride for him.'

'I heard tell that the W Bar G is the biggest ranch in these parts and its boss is pretty powerful,' commented Young.

'That's right. Walter Guisewell carved it out of nothing years ago when folks said this end of New Mexico could supply only rattlesnakes and dry seasons and was the damnedest place to start up a cattle outfit.'

'I'll say it is,' agreed Young. 'Making a desert-edge spread into a roaring success is a good trick. I reckon Mr Guisewell must be a man with brains and ability.'

Pete Hazen smiled sardonically.

'Oh, he is. No question about it. He gets things done efficiently when he sets his mind to it. Yes, sir, I guess there's no man in this territory to touch him for efficiency.'

Young jerked his head towards the batwing doors at his back.

'Is that hotel right across the street – the Mesa House – the only place here a man can find accommodation?' he asked.

'It's all Blue Mesa can offer,' Hazen told him. 'It's either a bunk in the Mesa House or your bedroll under the stars.'

'Then I reckon I'll be putting up there,' said Young. He already knew about the Mesa House. His brother Dick had stayed there and sent letters from that address.

Pete Hazen, sounding as if he was venturing on dangerous ground, asked cautiously:

'What brings you to Blue Mesa, Mr Young?'

'Oh, just visiting for a spell.' The answer sounded casual, but to Hazen and his companions it seemed to contain a veiled threat. Glances of suspicion darted between the whole W Bar G crew. In particular, the squat man with the

17

sparse moustache looked troubled and. again, his mouth twitched.

Young was wondering how soon this bunch of Guisewell's riders would be hotfooting it back to the rancher to report that the brother of the missing Dick Young was in town and that he bore all the marks of a gunslinger. He kept up his line of easy conversation with Hazen, asking:

'Are there stables over at the hotel, where a horse can be attended to?'

'Sure. Rube Cousins who runs the place has a set of stables in back.'

'Good. I'll get on over there and see that the cayuse is fed and watered.' Young sipped his beer slowly, then said in his casual style:

'I understand Blue Mesa does not have a newspaper.'

'No, nobody ever set up a paper here,' responded Hazen.

'A pity. A paper adds to the community spirit, but I'm told there is one in the town down the trail a piece, Sandy Crossing.'

Pete Hazen looked at him suspiciously.

'Sure, Sandy Crossing has one.'

'Good. I'll take a trip over there tomorrow. I'd like to have a notice published.'

Young still held his partly filled schooner in his left hand. He drained it in a couple of quick gulps, then placed the empty glass on the bar. The W Bar G men noted that he kept his right hand hovering over his pistol the whole time. Nodding to the crew of cowhands, he said:

'I'm obliged to you fellows.' Then he turned and strode for the door. He could almost feel the eyes of Guisewell's men watching his back as he departed.

Now, he thought, *you have the measure of me; you know who I am and where I'll be staying and you're all itching to know why I should be 'just visiting' the country where my brother rode out and vanished like last year's snow.*

CHAPTER THREE

'HERE TO FIND THE TRUTH'

Bob Young unhitched his rein from the saloon's hitch rail, which his horse had been sharing with the mounts of the W Bar G riders, and walked the animal over the dusty street towards the Mesa House. There, he secured it to the hotel's empty hitch rail, took his war sack from behind his saddle and strode into a narrow lobby.

It was no better and no worse than many hotels he had known along the frontier. Here and there the floor had drifts of the invasive brown, sandy dust commonly found in New Mexico that had blown in from the street. Otherwise the place looked reasonably clean.

Behind a rickety desk an old man with a face resembling wrinkled parchment seemed to be asleep, but he opened one eye to observe Young advancing on him. He looked hard at the newcomer and it was plain that the significance of the tied-down holster was not lost on him.

'Want to register, mister?' he asked, coupling a hopeful

note in the question with a hint of caution that was doubt-less due to the sight of the tied-down holster.

'Sure thing. I guess for a week to start with. And I want my horse feeding, watering and bedding down.'

'OK. I'll take care of that for you after I get you settled. I do pretty well everything around here myself.' He shoved a register towards Young then pushed an inkwell and pen to join it. 'I guess you'll have the run of the place. There are no other guests.'

Young noticed a suggestion of regretful resignation in this observation and remembered how a letter from Dick had mentioned that the Mesa House seemed to be always lacking guests. Apparently, this town hardly attracted visitors.

The old-timer looked at the signature after Young signed and his eyebrows rose. He eyed his new guest narrowly.

'Name of Young,' he commented. 'A young fellow of that name stayed here some time back.'

'I know. He was my brother,' said Young.

The old man shot him a look that seemed to be partly scared and partly crestfallen, then he shook his head.

'Pleasant young fellow. A real gentleman. Clever artist, too, I gather. What happened to him was a damned shame. He just plain disappeared, I heard.'

'It was a shame,' responded Young without emotion. 'You'll be Rube Cousins. My brother mentioned you in a couple of letters he wrote.'

'He did, did he?' Again, there was the look suggesting some kind of fear, then the old man asked quickly, as if wanting to change the subject, 'You got any preferences where your room is concerned? I have a pretty wide selection.'

'I'd like one overlooking the street.'

'That'll be easy. I'll put you in number two, just at the top of the stairs, on the left.'

'Do you lay on meals?' Young enquired.

'No. Most folk who stay here generally eat at the Ace Café, right across the street.' The old-timer gave an ironic chuckle and added, 'It's more accurate to say they *always* eat there. There's no other place in town. Anyway, they eat well. Cooty Sawkins who owns the café is a darned good cook.'

'In that case I'll follow the example of your other guests – when you have any – and sample his grub.' Young now adopted a conversational tone and added, 'It's kind of strange that not many folk visit Blue Mesa. Can it be that it is not exactly a boom town? Are there no people flocking in, attracted by its future possibilities when every other community in the West is hollering about the big opportunities it can offer new settlers?'

Rube Cousins shrugged and looked sorrowful.

'That's what was hoped for years ago when this end of New Mexico was opening up to settlers and I was tempted to shift from Texas and invest my all, setting up this place. But – well, I guess none of it worked out right. You might say there were forces acting against prosperity hitting Blue Mesa.'

He turned to take a key from a board behind the desk. 'I'll show you to your room, Mr Young.'

Cousins came from behind the desk and led the way to the stairs that led up from one side of the lobby. Young followed him, carrying his war sack.

The room was small and neat with a narrow bed in one corner and a small dressing table. Young took a quick look out of the window and found it gave a good view of the opposite side of the street. He dumped his war sack on the bed.

'I reckon this room will suit me just fine,' he said. Rube Cousins gave a nervous laugh.

'Maybe I should have told you this was the room your brother had,' he said.

'All to the good,' approved Young. 'He told me in one of his letters that he was settled right comfortably in his hotel. I reckon his recommendation was good.'

When Cousins had left him he looked from the window again. He could see the Lucky Dollar saloon, and at that moment the W Bar G hands, led by Pete Hazen, trooped out through its portals and headed for their hitched horses.

One man, however, a short, weasel-faced individual, detached himself from the group and strode off along the boardwalk to a wooden structure over the door of which a board declared it to be the office of the city marshal.

Young saw, at one corner of his field of vision, the riders moving off in a cloud of dust, while at the other corner he saw their detached colleague disappear into the office of the lawman. He gave a wry smile to think that the bulk of the W Bar G men were en route to acquaint their boss with the news that the brother of missing Dick Young had turned up and that one of their number had hastened away to relay the information to the marshal.

'Blue Mesa sure is a well-ordered town,' he murmured to himself. 'A tight little community where news, good or bad, travels fast and all the important people are well informed in no time at all.'

He turned from the window and looked around the room. So this was where Dick had spent the days before he vanished! Here he had written the couple of letters to his brother that Bob Young had in his wallet at that moment. They told him plenty but the recipient wanted to know very much more.

It was from here that Dick set off on his last journey to the place his letter said was known as Crouching Lion. It seemed the location took its name from a natural rock formation beside a deep chasm. To the Apache, native to this area for centuries, its shape suggested a mountain lion crouching in readiness to spring into the chasm and attack some prey.

It seemed there were ancient, tangled and half-understood superstitions associated with both the rock formation and the dried-up chasm over which it kept its eternal, menacing watch.

Dick's letter gave no indication of why he was going to Crouching Rock. Whether or not it was to keep a specific rendezvous, his journey ended with him disappearing into total oblivion. His horse, it seemed, was hazed away and never seen again.

'Well, Dick, I'm here to find the truth of what happened – and I'll make good and sure I don't finish up missing!'

With this vow Young descended the stairs and found that Rube Cousins was no longer in the lobby. A plump Mexican woman was dusting down the desk and he remembered how Dick had written that Cousins largely ran the place, with only a Mexican widow as general helper.

'Boss fixing your horse,' she said, jerking her head towards the back of the premises. 'I'm Rosita. Your room OK?'

'Yes, OK. You can tell Mr Cousins I've stepped across to the café for a meal.'

She nodded and, with an impassive expression, watched him walk out of the door.

Crossing the street, Young noted how it was just as lacking in citizenry as when he first rode into town. Even allowing for the blazing sun and the heavy, breezeless air, Blue Mesa seemed to be remarkably bereft of any spark of vitality.

With the W Bar G riders departed, all the remaining hitch rails on the street were without horses, but one mount was still tethered outside the Lucky Dollar. It was that of the ranch hand, who was obviously still in the marshal's office.

There were no parked wagons or carriages; no bustle of people going about their business; no people standing around in conversation – and no energetic children. There was simply nothing typifying a properly functioning town.

Young recalled Rube Cousins's remark about bright prospects failing to reach fruition in Blue Mesa.

Plainly, the town was out of kilter with the driving spirit of the rest of the expanding West.

The nineteenth century was reaching its end and vast changes were occurring. The long-anticipated flowering of promise in the previously untamed lands beyond the western horizon was beginning to burgeon.

Not long ago, up on the northern ranges, the blizzards of ceaseless snow in the murderous winter of 1886-87 had caused men and cattle to freeze to death. Graze blanketed by feet of snow was unattainable and stock was reduced to pathetic near-skeletons, floundering blindly in snowdrifts. Prairie wolves circled the doomed creatures, eager for the kill.

Ranchers rapidly went broke, cowhands were laid off

and too many, penniless through lack of work, turned to crime.

That winter went into folklore as 'The Great Die-up' and there were those who believed nature was putting paid to old-style open-range ranching. Maybe the new, go-getting land and cattle companies would soon dominate beef-raising.

The old-time veterans, used to the open ranges and the long, hard years of round-ups and of driving herds to the railheads, began to lose faith in the routine of a life they had long taken for granted. Maybe the old order was dying.

Yet progress still marched onward with confidence in the West.

Railroads furthered their reach and ore-mining boomed in some regions. In others, there was excitement at the discovery of oil and there was a national feeling that an era of widespread industry was about to dawn, bringing a new bonanza of prosperity.

Bob Young was acutely aware of advancing change. Soon, he thought, his own breed, the Western phenomenon of the man with a tied-down holster, would pass away.

What he saw with his own eyes, together with the comments of Rube Cousins and the revelations of Dick's letters, led him to believe that even while the Western territories boomed vigorously, Blue Mesa remained entirely untouched by the regional experience of progress.

As Young expected, he found the Ace Café empty of customers. It seemed it was blighted by the same lack of vitality as he'd found at the hotel. Though it was obviously spotlessly kept its tables were surely laid for customers who would never arrive.

Cooty Sawkins proved to be a man of small build as he

emerged from the back premises to appear at the counter with an air of surprise at finding a customer in the place. His eyes flew to the holster tied down at Young's thigh and his air of surprise changed to one of nervous suspicion.

'What'll it be?' he asked somewhat querulously.

'Rube Cousins, over at the hotel, tells me you're a top-hand cook, so I'll settle for what you can serve up in the way of meat, potatoes, vegetables and coffee,' responded Young with open amiability. Sawkins looked brighter.

'Well that was right neighbourly of Rube. I reckon I can settle your appetite easily enough, sir,' he said; then he hurried back to the rear quarters.

Young seated himself at a table and thought how his first impressions of Blue Mesa bore out the descriptions of the town and its pervading spirit given in the couple of long letters sent by Dick.

Old Cousins had referred to forces that worked against prosperity ever hitting Blue Mesa and Bob Young had detected in Cooty Sawkins the same resigned acceptance of failure as that displayed by the hotel keeper.

He guessed that both men, when young, had staked everything on Blue Mesa's proving to be another spectacular frontier town, fat with opportunities for generating wealth. It had been a false hope and the two men, now ageing, were stuck with struggling businesses.

He felt that both Cousins and Sawkins could be made to open up on some hidden truths concerning Blue Mesa and the forces at work in it – if he could win the confidence of the pair.

CHAPTER FOUR

GUNFIGHTER'S REPUTATION

At about the time that Bob Young sat down to his meal in the Ace Café the W Bar G riders led by Pete Hazen reached the Split Rock Sink, a location where a fresh-water spring fed a pool guarded by rocks and a set of spindly live oaks.

This was a stopover on the way to the W Bar G ranch, where travellers could water their horses and themselves and take time for a smoke.

The riders dismounted, led their animals to the pool and slaked their own thirst before allowing the horses to drink.

Just as Pete Hazen was wiping his mouth with the back of his hand after taking several satisfying gulps, Slim Forster, a skinny, gangling hand, approached him. He looked as if he was keeping the lid clamped down on something exciting.

'Pete, awhile back I realized there's something I must tell you about that Young joker,' he announced breathlessly.

'Yeah? What is it?' asked Hazen.

'As soon as I saw him I figured I knew him from some-where else. I guess the sight of him plumb scared me and I was kind of stunned. Then, just a little ways back along the trail it came to me that he was for certain the man I thought he was – and he's pure poison.'

Hazen's hand froze close to his shirt pocket as he was reaching for the makings to roll a cigarette, and his ample moustache bristled.

'It's took you long enough to get it off your chest, but tell me more,' he demanded angrily.

'Well, he was deputy marshal of Twin Boulders, Wyoming, when I hung around there before coming to New Mexico. Only, in those days, he was known as Hank Teed. He had that same, edgy style with his hand – always ready to snatch his gun. You knew he was trouble as soon as you clapped eyes on him.

'The story was that he was once part of the Alonzo Keller gang that was cleared up in Arizona a few years before. He was known to have served time in that damned hell hole in Yuma, Arizona. He came out all reformed and took up law enforcement. He worked under Lew Conners, the marshal of Twin Boulders, who was a tough customer. Teed was just as tough but quieter and more thoughtful. But he could use his gun. I recall how he once settled a hell of a saloon fight all on his lonesome.

'It started with fists then it turned to gunplay. Hot lead was flying every whichway when Teed busted in – shooting. He made the place peaceable in no time at all and three troublemakers were left dead on the floor. I know for sure Young is Teed and he's pretty damned quick on the trigger.'

'Any man with a tied-down holster advertises that fact,'

grunted Hazen sourly. 'Too bad you didn't remember all of this before we sent Shorty Dix in to confab with Marshal Todd. Todd should know what he might be up against.' He paused and made a wry face, then added, 'I know Todd and he's no match for a slick gunsharp.'

'Hell, Pete, the sight of him just bulldogged me. I didn't rightly collect myself until we were well on the trail,' explained Forster.

'Well, there's no question but what this Bob Young is the brother of Dick Young. That family resemblance is no coincidence,' growled Hazen. 'He came here making it plain as day he's one of the gunfighter breed and he's out to make trouble. Back in the Lucky Dollar, he looked ready to start it then and there, in spite of his smooth talk.'

'After what happened to his brother I guess that's understandable,' drawled a languid voice from the back of the knot of men surrounding Hazen and Forster.

The whole party, apparently struck by shock, swung around to stare at the speaker, Cal Davis. He was a lugubrious, slack-jawed Texan who usually gave the impression of being half-asleep. He had only recently joined the Guisewell outfit. He kept a close mouth and none of the crew knew anything of his history.

'Hey, don't let me hear you say anything of that kind again,' snarled Pete Hazen. 'And make good and sure Mr Guisewell never hears that sort of talk from you. Keep your face shut, Davis. Always keep it shut good and tight!'

Cal Davis shrugged and resumed his habitual expression of not being much interested in what was going on around him. Hazen singled out the paunchy man with the straggling moustache.

'And, while we're on the subject, you, Anderson, get a

hold on your reactions. You almost prodded Young into cutting loose on you in the saloon and I'm damned sure he would have blown half a dozen holes in you before you got your gun clear of leather.'

Pete Hazen was obviously affected by the information of which Slim Forster had just unburdened himself. He had abandoned his rolling of the smoke, and now he would allow no one else there a break for tobacco.

'C'mon, the whole bunch of you. We have to move quick, we can't linger here,' he barked.

The ranch hands stared at him without budging. This weather was of the kind that made old greybeards predict that, when heat built up in this way in New Mexico, it invariably broke in some spectacular way. Sweaty and menacing, the atmosphere told on riders after relatively few miles, and the men were hankering for a rest and a smoke at the sink.

'Jump to it, dammit!' hooted Hazen. 'Get those cayuses away from the water and mount up. We have business back at the W Bar G.'

Walter Guisewell stood on the long gallery fronting the substantial ranch house of the W Bar G. His eyes were focused on a set of moving blobs behind a shimmering curtain of heat haze on the far horizon. Gradually they grew larger, more distinct and became recognizable as horses and riders.

'Here they come,' muttered the rancher. 'I gave them a few hours to go to town for some relaxation but if one of them shows up drunk I'll have the hide off him.'

Guisewell was tall and craggy and as mean as he had been on the day he came into this raw and obscure portion of the great American desert as a young man determined to make his pile. He had made his pile and become a power in the land but prosperity had not given him a paunch or fancy manners.

His face, seamed and burned by years of exposure to a harsh sun, bore a spiky longhorn moustache made white by age and his expression was one of permanent discontent. He wore range garb with a Colt Peacemaker belted at his waist. He still roped, branded and cussed with his cowhands and he ruled the W Bar G with a rod of iron.

He was not loved by the hands but they respected and obeyed him. He kept their loyalty by paying good wages and he was known to tolerate even men with spotty reputations without asking questions about past exploits provided they understood that he was in command of pretty well every breath they took.

Recent years, having been particularly harsh, had brought a good number of men who sought warmer climates down to this region nudging the border with Mexico.

Several disillusioned and tight-lipped individuals had drifted down from the northern ranges of Montana and Wyoming some years back, after the 'Big Die-up' had worked wholesale misery on men and beasts.

They had good reason to thank Walter Guisewell for his high wages and most were indifferent to the fact that their loyalty had been bought. There were dangerous hardcases riding as working wranglers for Guisewell and, in past instances, he had made good use of them. They formed a squad of tough enforcers of his will in ruling what, like some arrogant king, he called his 'country'. It was they who, when required, provided muscle in keeping what Guisewell called 'order' in Blue Mesa. The town's marshal and his deputy were merely token officers.

Only those people who had been in the Blue Mesa locality for a fair span of years could recall how genuine love had once entered the life of the young Walter Guisewell. He had brought a youthful bride to the pioneering cattle spread, which he was creating with a vigorous determination that brought him respect for all his toughness.

In no time at all fever carried the young woman off and it was then that steel entered Guisewell's soul. Life, which he had once embraced so enthusiastically, savouring all its opportunities and gifts, had played him false. It had robbed him of the only human creature he ever fully loved.

So he vowed he would take on the treacherous enemy called either life or fate and fight it as if it was a wild beast. He would squeeze out everything it had to offer in the way of material compensation, particularly every dollar and every last red cent.

He determined to exploit it to make his pile ever higher. He would take good care never to be hurt by that enemy again.

Guisewell watched the returning horsemen pound into the ranch yard. Pete Hazen spurred his mount to take him ahead of his companions and pulled rein in front of the gallery. His face was grave and he was brimming with news.

On the ride in the men had agreed not to tell Guisewell anything of Fats Anderson's tentative move to draw and his backing down. It was best to keep the rancher in ignorance of any W Bar G hand's attempting to start gunplay when in town. Hazen addressed the rancher from the saddle, yelling loudly and excitedly:

'The brother of Dick Young has showed up in town.

He looks like a regular gunslinger. Forster here remembers him from Wyoming. Forster says he has a reputation and was with the Alonzo Keller gang in Arizona. Forster reckons he's plenty dangerous and he sure enough looks like trouble.'

'The hell you say?' grunted Guisewell. 'Well, don't sit there hollering from your horse fit to bring the house down. Come inside and bring Forster with you.'

The foreman and Forster dismounted and marched into the well-appointed living room of the house, where Guisewell confronted them, frowning and with angry eyes.

'What's this about a gunslinging brother of Dick Young?' he demanded harshly.

'Oh, he's a gunslinger all right, Mr Guisewell,' answered Pete Hazen. 'Every aspect of his style and his attitude advertised it. Forster, here, knew him up in Wyoming.'

'And he's a powerful dangerous proposition, Mr Guisewell,' put in Forster in a jittery voice. Guisewell glowered at Forster.

'Sounds like you're scared of him, Forster,' he said scornfully. 'You should know well enough who calls the tune in these parts. No damned trigger-tripper comes into Blue Mesa or any other part of Walt Guisewell's country and throws his weight around. There's a quick cure waiting for those who try it, as he'll find out soon enough.'

Forster, with his first-hand knowledge of Young as a gunslinger, looked distinctly disturbed and shook his head.

'With respect, Mr Guisewell, I don't think it'll be easy to settle his hash,' he ventured. The rancher snorted.

'Forster, get this through your head; I hold the whip hand in this country and if any smart joker comes in and shoves his nose into where it's not wanted, I'm the man to put him in his place – you can be damned sure of it.'

Pete Hazen pulled at his ginger moustache thoughtfully.

'Young has something up his sleeve, Mr Guisewell,' he said. 'He was talking about putting some sort of notice in the Sandy Crossing newspaper.'

'Oh, was he? I wonder what that means? The paper is published Wednesday, isn't it?'

Hazen agreed that it was.

'That's the day after tomorrow,' Guisewell said: He turned to Forster and ordered sharply, 'Forster, ride over to Sandy Crossing first thing Wednesday morning and collect a copy of the paper. From what you two tell me, Young swaggered into town prodding for trouble. I don't know what his aim is in putting a notice in the paper, but, with his damned cocky attitude, it seems he might just as well have put up posters saying he was here to bring a showdown.'

Guisewell paused, pushed out his chin belligerently, slammed his right fist into the palm of his left hand and spat:

'I'm good and riled by Young. You can put it around the crew in the bunkhouse that they better oil up their shooting irons – because a hell of a showdown could well be coming up!'

CHAPTER FIVE

NEWS IN SANDY CROSSING

The township of Sandy Crossing was a distance of six horseback miles from Blue Mesa. When Young, with a certain caution in his voice, sought directions to it from Rube Cousins, the hotel owner mentioned that a slight diversion from the main trail could allow him to pass Crouching Lion, the location for which his brother was supposedly heading when he vanished.

'That's mighty interesting,' said Young. 'I intend to look at that country as soon as I can. Might just as well do it as I pass that way.'

He rode off under a brassy morning sun that promised to slam many more hours of heat upon the terrain, and eventually he came to the spot where a lesser trail offered a diversion from the main trail to the town.

He followed it into a stretch of arid country where there was a jagged wall of rock rising to one side of the trail. The wall contained a number of dark openings that were obviously caves.

Then he saw the hulking rock formation rising up further along the trail, on the side opposite the rocky wall. The formation on which the wind had worked for innumerable centuries had the uncannily natural semblance of a mountain lion, ready to spring into the deep chasm that split the ground directly beneath it.

Young halted his mount and looked along the trail as it passed under Crouching Lion.

He put to himself the proposal that Dick had been bushwhacked somewhere near here and his body thrown into the chasm.

He looked at the rising rocks, boulders and caves across the trail and opposite Crouching Lion. Anywhere along that rugged margin, an ambusher – or more than one – could lie concealed, ready to pick off with ease an unsuspecting horseman on the trail below.

He climbed down from the saddle, left his horse grazing on such sparse greenery as it could find sprouting among the rocks and walked over to the edge of the yawning gash of the chasm. He looked into depths that seemed bottomless.

Here and there rocky ledges jutted out on either side of the great cleft in the ground. Young, thinking of Dick's corpse being cast into those depths, realized that it might have fallen on to one of the ledges, but, intently though he stared in to the chasm he could see no body sprawled out on any of the ledges below.

A strong man, or maybe a couple acting as a team, would be needed to throw the corpse a considerable distance so that it kept well clear of the sides of the chasm as it fell out of sight.

As he stepped back from the edge of the chasm he

caught sight of a human being who seemed to have sprung from nowhere and was standing motionless close to the form of the crouching lion, watching him intently.

The man's lean body was the colour of copper. He wore only a breechcloth and had long black hair, which descended down his back; his brow was encircled by a broad headband. He was staring directly at Young, face unexpressive of any emotion. He looked as if he was defending the curious lion-like rock.

Young felt a jerk of alarm at his innards as he realized that this was an Apache. It was a reaction conditioned by the fierce reputation of the Apache people, whe until only recently had been seen as stubbornly and bloodthirstily opposed to settlers encroaching upon their domain.

He fought down the unease, knowing that the Apaches had been subdued and confined to reservations, though it was known that a few remained free, somehow managing to pursue their ancient ways and perhaps secretly guarding their old sacred places.

He moved towards the man, intending to speak to him, but even as he did so he found that the Apache had vanished as mysteriously as he had appeared.

Young cuffed back his sombrero and scratched his brow. He wondered whether the man had really been there, or had he been a phantom produced by the shimmering heat haze.

Puzzled, he remounted and resumed the main trail.

At length, he plodded into Sandy Crossing, a collection of adobe dwellings and shacks of sun-warped wood, sprawling on the sweltering flatlands.

Sandy Crossing was larger than Blue Mesa and every bit as

raw and ugly but, as Young noticed at once on riding into its single street, it had a throbbing vitality wholly lacking in the near defeated settlement he had departed from earlier.

Even on this morning of early torpid heat, there was movement. There were people, horses, wagons, carriages, and there was noise. The very aromas in the air signified that this town was wide awake and vigorously alive.

He found the office of the *Sandy Crossing Sentinel* on a crowded boardwalk, shaded by a wide awning. The name of the paper was emblazoned, newspaper masthead style, over the door and, added, was the legend: MIKE FRASER, PUBLISHER AND EDITOR.

He shoved open the door, entered and was met by the pungent smell of printers' ink. There was a hand-operated flatbed press in the shadowy background and, nearer to him, a long counter piled with newspapers.

There was also a woman behind the counter. She was neatly turned out and was strikingly and serenely good-looking. A few streaks of grey showed in her deftly arranged dark hair, indicating that she was no longer young. She was, perhaps, a few years junior to Young.

Young touched the brim of his hat to her and fumbled in his shirt pocket for a folded paper he had prepared the night before. He laid it on the counter.

'I'd like to place this in the next edition, ma'am,' he said. 'I don't know if you call it a public notice or what, but please tell me the cost.'

The woman read his handwriting:

Robert Young, visiting New Mexico, is staying in our neigh-bouring township, Blue Mesa for a few days. Our readers may recall hearing that, some time ago, his brother, Richard Young, a travelling artist, vanished, supposedly close to the landmark, Crouching Lion.

Robert Young, a former peace officer, indicates that he intends to look into matters surrounding the disappearance of his brother. He would appreciate any information, no matter how small, that local citizenry might be able to volunteer. He can be reached at the Mesa House, Blue Mesa.

Naturally, the text did not reveal that, before his career as a peace officer, Robert Young had served a lengthy term as a convict.

The woman looked at the text with wide eyes.

'Well, it's not quite in the usual run of things, but I guess it can be considered a family notice. You know, a notice that Mrs Someone has gone to visit her daughter in Albuquerque, or Mr and Mrs Somebody Else are planning to host a family reunion at their home. We don't charge for family notices so you can have this one printed free.'

'That's handsome, ma'am,' Young said.

She gave him a bright smile. 'My brother, Mike, the editor, says such notices are the lifeblood of small-town newspapers. They help fill space and he always says names make news and spread community spirit. We print tonight so you arrived just in time for this week's edition.'

For a moment she fell silent, then she tapped the paper Young had laid on the counter and said in a quieter tone:

'I'm sorry about your brother. I remember word of his disappearance going around. Some folks here met him when he was sketching in the locality. Blue Mesa and Crouching Lion are not part of our circulation area so we never covered the story. News of it drifted over to us but, as it happened off our territory, we did not follow it up by reporting it or any enquiries by the law.'

She looked at Young, gave an ironic smile and added, 'Maybe I should say what *passes* for the law in Blue Mesa.'

Her attractive eyes were cornflower-blue and they held a wise, frank look. This woman was no fool, thought Young. He returned the smile, nodded and said:

'Sure. I know exactly what you mean.'

The street door opened and a tall man stepped in. He wore a black broadcloth suit and a black sombrero. He was clean-shaven and his expression was thoughtful and intellectual. He looked like a man who might have been a young officer on one side or the other in the Civil War that had ended over twenty years before.

'Ah, here's my brother Mike now,' said the woman; she addressed the newcomer. 'Mike, this is Mr Young. His brother was the artist who disappeared somewhere near Crouching Lion some time back – you'll remember when that happened.'

Mike Fraser looked Young over, noting how his garb made him obviously a man of the outdoors. He did not miss the tied-down holster. His sister leaned across the counter and handed him the text that Young had prepared.

'Mr Young wants us to run this item,' she explained. Fraser read the notice and nodded approval.

'Sure, we'll run it,' he commented. He addressed Young, 'That affair concerning your brother was damned peculiar. I didn't know him myself but I heard he did some sketching out this way and some townsfolk met him. I was thinking of hunting him out and doing a story on him. Civilized visitors like artists are kind of rare. However, he seemed to have disappeared and folks began to wonder.'

He gave a frustrated sort of sigh and added, 'I guess he was waylaid, robbed and killed and his body and horse were disposed of. An artist innocently recording the picturesque elements of New Mexico was surely unlikely to be harming anybody.'

Young nodded agreement, though he knew Dick's activities were hardly the innocent ones that Mike Fraser imagined.

Then Mike Fraser made an observation that caused Young to catch his breath.

'The disappearance of your brother was worrying because it was not the first time such a thing had happened,' said the editor.

This sharpened Young's thirst for information, but for the moment he wanted to follow another line of enquiry.

CHAPTER SIX

DISAPPEARANCES

Young asked Mike Fraser a question the answer to which he considered vital.

'Do you know of any legal steps taken after my brother disappeared?'

Fraser frowned. 'Well, I guess some report was made to Ezra Todd, town marshal of Blue Mesa, since he was the nearest officer of the law. All the legalities should have been followed by him, but because the affair did not occur in our legal district, I never learned anything about it.'

'From all I hear about Guisewell, I guess he has a way of making things work out his way, and that might go for the law in his bailiwick', said Young. 'Away out in the far end of a territory like New Mexico, it's probably easy to bypass the statutes of the United States.'

'I think you're near the mark there,' said the editor. 'You've spent some time in Blue Mesa and got the feel of the place?'

'I spent only one night there so far but it was long

enough to give me a fair impression.'

'You'll soon see that the whole town is blighted,' Fraser said forcefully. 'Every time I've visited I've felt it was gripped by something that had all but squeezed the vitality and verve out of the place. But it's not gripped by something but *someone* – and he's Walt Guisewell. If anyone knows what goes on around that town, it's Guisewell.'

Fraser warmed to the subject, 'I don't deny the man had enterprise at first, He created that town and built most of it. He owns fistfuls of property on its street but he thinks his word is law. There is no real town council and Marshal Todd and his deputy are in Guisewell's pocket. Guisewell acts as if he has an empire at his feet, but he's so blamed stubborn he can't see that the old times are slipping away fast.'

'I guess you've got him sized up right, Mr Fraser,' said Young. 'I figure Blue Mesa suffers from his presence rather than benefits from it.'

'Sure, when he was younger and the town was in its infancy, he was in favour of some business development,' Fraser replied. 'But then he clamped down on anyone showing any real enterprise. I thought of starting a paper there once but I quickly took account of Guisewell's attitude. I knew he'd be out to take control of it.'

Fraser's sister smiled at Young. 'You must excuse Mike's excitement,' she said. 'He's an enthusiast for the freedom of the press and he sometimes gets preachy on the subject.'

'And why not, Charlotte?' demanded her brother. 'Too many politicians and vested interests try to control newspapers to make them serve their own purposes. But, by thunder, an unfettered press is a hallmark of a healthy democracy. I'm damned if I'd allow Guisewell to crush the spirit of any paper I edited.'

'I agree with you, Mr Fraser,' Young said. 'I've met people in Blue Mesa who seem to be totally dispirited by the atmosphere of the place.'

He was thinking of Rube Cousins and Cooty Sawkins, both of whom obviously shared the defeatism engendered by Guisewell's heavy-handedness and who seemed to have been browbeaten into timidity. Fraser nodded,

'Guisewell's surrounded himself with a set of hard-cases, some of them said to be on the dodge from elsewhere, but their day is passing as quickly as his own. The W Bar G is their last bolt-hole. Have you visited Crouching Lion, where your brother was rumoured to be headed for?'

'I looked in on it when passing on the way here. I'd like to know more about it.'

'A strange and sinister place of legends,' said Fraser. 'The Apaches fear it but, at the same time, see it as favoured by the spirits and believe that it occasionally brings the blessing of water into the desert.

'As an old apparent water course, the chasm has been dry seemingly almost since time began. But, Indian super-stition says there are times when it fills up with rushing water which overflows to fill the parched land. This is good medicine, worked by the benevolent spirits. The Apaches are subdued now and a johnny-come-lately like Guisewell claims ownership of their sacred lion and supposed water course, though it's doubtful if his lands stretch that far.' Fraser paused and waved towards the window.

'Think of that wild land yonder,' he stated. 'The Apaches knew more about it than we do, but we dismiss their wisdom too easily even though we are only recent intruders and conquerors.'

Young found his thoughts returning to the apparition he thought he'd seen at Crouching Lion – of an Apache who seemed to be guarding the natural sculpture.

Charlotte Fraser intruded with a peal of laughter, which to Young was enchanting.

'Mike is riding another hobby horse, Mr Young,' she said. 'He's keen to know everything about the history of the land and the people who were once here.'

'And so we should,' replied her brother. 'A place gets a ghostly reputation which usually indicates that some incident happened there long in the past. If we knew the truth behind the tales clinging to Crouching Lion, we'd have clues to the detailed history of the Apaches who have no written record of their own.'

Young knew exactly what he meant. He had lived in wild places but was always aware of a mystic set of lifeways existing just beyond a thin curtain of time.

Sometimes the mysterious past was glimpsed through the discovery of a shard of exquisite pottery created by a people who had never discovered the wheel. Or perhaps through a vague weather-worn pictograph carved on an ancient rock or through bones of unknowable age found buried in the desert with artefacts suggesting some unknown funeral ceremony.

Mike Fraser gave an ironic laugh and observed, 'We think we're pretty darned smart but we can't untangle the background of the ancient people any more than we can solve modern mysteries like the case of the two men who vanished like your brother somewhere near Crouching Lion some time back.'

Young looked at him with an alert expression and

remembered how Fraser had earlier referred to some such happening.

'Two men disappeared?' he asked quickly. 'When was that?'

'Only a short time before your brother vanished.'

This was weighty information. Bob Young knew that his brother was something other than a footloose artist, picturing the desert landscapes. He had been in this region for another, unrevealed purpose. Mike Fraser's revelation caused Young to conjecture that the purpose was the investigation of the disappearance of the two men.

'And you say it happened somewhere around Crouching Lion?' he asked.

'Well, that was what people figured,' said Fraser. 'I never met the pair but they passed through here and it transpired they had booked rooms at our hotel. I understand they were youngish and looked brainy. Some folks felt they might be army officers out of uniform, but who knows? They never occupied those hotel rooms. They rode out right after booking them, having asked the way to Crouching Lion. After that, they were never seen again. Nor were the horses they hired from a livery stable right here in town.'

Young rubbed his chin thoughtfully. This nugget of information was an enlightening bonus to the reason for his visit to the newspaper office. It made the purpose for Dick's mission in New Mexico plain to Bob Young. It was to investigate the disappearance of the two men and, in following his commission, Dick had also disappeared.

Bob liked Mike Fraser and his sister. He judged them the most stimulating people he had so far met in New Mexico, in contrast to his acquaintances in Blue Mesa: the dangerous-looking W Bar G hands in the saloon and the timid Rube Cousins and Cooty Sawkins.

'I'll be moving on,' he said, extending a hand to the editor. 'It was pleasant to make your acquaintance, Mr Fraser.' He looked towards the woman at the counter and, almost guiltily, found himself looking at her hands which were in view. There was no wedding ring.

'Yours, too, Miss Fraser,' he said.

She did not correct him as to her title and, being unaccustomed to dealing with women, he felt elatedly that there was a rare second bonus in the brightness of her cornflower-blue eyes as she smiled at him and said softly:

'Goodbye, Mr Young, and good luck with everything.'

Returning to Blue Mesa, he thought of the attractive blue eyes of Charlotte Fraser and her friendly personality. He wondered why such a fine-looking woman should remain unmarried for so long. Maybe there was a suitor in the past, perhaps one who perished in the destructive Civil War.

'All of that's none of your damned business,' he admonished himself out loud.

But the memory of the woman lingered on his mind.

He followed the trail back to Blue Mesa under a sun blazing more fiercely than ever. The still, oven-like heat of the air was even more heavily oppressive and it seemed that it would last for ever.

The reduced level of a small streamlet where he halted to rest and water his mount gave an ominous forecast. Soon, all the land would be crying out for water.

Back at the Mesa House he drank a welcome draught of water, exercising a desert man's caution in not taking too much after a long spell under so gruelling a sun; then he took out his wallet and lay on his bed.

From the wallet, he took the carefully preserved letters from Dick that had sparked off his present venture. He had read them many times but now he unfolded them and began to read once more.

Sight of the handwriting of his late brother brought back in a rush of nostalgia the feel of the days of his youth when he and Dick had lived as youngsters in an environment that was hardly peaceable, but their family life was tranquil and enjoyable.

That was before war split the nation apart and the brothers, in their early manhood, were plunged deep into a nightmare of killing and despoiling.

CHAPTER SEVEN

THE STORY OF
BOB YOUNG

Though his youth had hardly been troubled, Bob Young could now see that conflicting currents surged in him without his fully appreciating it.

He and his brother were the sons of a farmer who had moved with his family from Virginia into turbulent Kansas just before that region became a bubbling cauldron of shootings, riots, and the destruction of property perpetrated by two factions: those who wanted to retain and expand slavery in Kansas and Missouri, and those who wanted to end the enslavement of human beings.

This blood-soaked period had been simply a rehearsal for the coming Civil War, which exploded soon after Abraham Lincoln was elected President of the United States.

That war swallowed young men such as Bob and Dick Young. Energetic and adventurous Bob followed his conscience and joined Lincoln's Union army for, in his youthful idealism, he had long been won over by the arguments against slavery propounded by the North under Lincoln's leadership.

Dick, older by a couple of years and following the same philosophy, had earlier rallied to the Union cause and also joined the blue-clad army. He served in another regiment and, being always deployed on different fronts, the brothers never met during the four years of war.

Their decision to serve under the Union flag rather than that of the rebel South angered and embittered their Southern-born father, who could not turn his back on his native Virginia. Having lost his wife a few years before, and already in indifferent health, he was left to cope with the farm alone. He survived for a couple of years into the war and died unreconciled to his sons. Both were then on faraway battlefields.

The fortunes of war which produced horrifying casualty lists largely favoured the brothers, who fought through numerous engagements. Bob received minor wounds in two of the actions: a mini-ball through the calf of one leg, and a cheek slashed by shrapnel, which left him with a scar.

Dick fared better in spite of many experiences on the hellish battlefields. In all his service he suffered nothing more than a severe bout of fever brought on by foul camp conditions. He survived it and was hurled back into action.

He had been a natural artist since boyhood and the army employed his artistic skills. He made risky excursions ahead of Union lines to sketch Confederate fortifications and possible routes of approach for attacking purposes. He progressed in artistic prowess.

After the war Bob Young was, like many another young ex-soldier, unanchored, without a home and schooled in little but armed aggression. He drifted to the expanding frontier, tried several jobs without finding satisfaction and became proficient with the Colt revolver, so popular with the more reckless and lawless denizens of the West.

Almost before he knew it he was caught up in the post-war savagery rife among young, rootless ex-soldiers. He used the gun as a tool of his trade, riding with a collection of bank robbers and cattle rustlers, mostly made up of veterans of both Civil War armies. He took the name of Hank Teed, conscious that he was violating the traditions of his respectable family. The leader of the gang he ran with was a fierce enemy of law and order, a former Confederate colonel named Alonzo Keller, who was totally unreconciled to the post-war law of the Yankees.

Bob's battlefield good luck held out through several wild, bullet-bitten incidents in the south-west until the gang was cornered by a determined squad of peace officers and civilian vigilantes in a canyon in Arizona.

He was not hurt in the furious exchange of fire between the two factions but, when the gunsmoke cleared, several on both sides were dead, including Alonzo Keller. The survivors of his gang were put under arrest.

During his sojourn with the Keller outfit, Bob Young had expended plenty of bullets, but he meticulously guarded against deliberately taking life. At the trial, a succession of witnesses to the gang's various raids gave evidence which resulted in several of its members being hanged. The rest drew sentences in the Arizona territorial prison at Yuma.

Bob Young, against whom there was never a charge of murder, had been among the imprisoned.

The prison at Yuma was no bed of roses. It was a brutal

establishment located in one of the most parched regions of Arizona Territory, but Young stoically served out his time. In the course of it he found a belated maturity. He was grateful for coming out of so many dangers with a whole skin and he realized that he was glad to be alive even if he was constrained by iron bars and the shackles frequently employed at Yuma.

As never before, he saw that if he continued on his previous course his luck would finally run out; he might easily end his life branded as a murderer and being lowered into an unhallowed grave, quite likely with a neck marked by the hangman's rope.

He was released from Yuma with a firm resolution concerning his future. He also had regrets. He regretted that he had kept out of touch with his father throughout the Civil War. Despite their political differences, his father had been a good parent to Dick and himself.

He felt guilty for not being on hand when his father died and for ending up in prison, which his father would see as a disgrace. Also, he was anxious for news of Dick. He did not know whether he had survived the war.

About the future, he was certain: he was going straight.

He could rejoice at being spared to have a future and he was determined that his future would be more valuable and worth while than his past of frontier hellraising in a fog of gunsmoke and desperate horseback chases while holding on to his precarious life by the skin of his teeth.

On his release he was determined to discover whether his brother was alive. He returned to Kansas, located an old neighbour, formerly an officer in Dick's former Union Army regiment, who verified that Dick lived. The neighbour knew that he was an investigator for a private detective agency based in Denver, Colorado, a city still growing and gathering energetic men speculating in railroad development and westward expansion.

The ex-officer wrote a character reference for Dick when he applied for the post. By a stroke of luck he could supply Bob with the address of the agency.

Bob Young wrote to his brother, care of the agency, and was duly heartened by a reply from Dick, now residing in Denver.

Dick's first letter was enthusiastic about a reunion of the brothers after the rigours of the war, but it revealed almost nothing about his work as an investigator for the detective agency. In one paragraph there was a veiled suggestion that there was something highly secretive about it.

Bob wanted to take a trip to Denver but there was a matter of cost. The small amount of money he had brought out of Yuma, earned by paid labour in prison, was dwindling. He needed cash.

Then he heard of an opportunity in Twin Boulders, Wyoming, where the town marshal, Lew Conners, was looking for a deputy.

Settling in Twin Boulders, Wyoming, would mean he was reasonably close to Denver. He had hopes of accruing funds by working as deputy marshal, so enabling him to travel on to Denver and be reunited with his brother.

There was a snag. Marshal Lew Conners had a frontier-wide reputation as a hard man among peace officers: he might well reject a candidate who had served time in prison and had a reputation as gun-fighting Hank Teed.

Using the last of his slim finances, Bob journeyed to Twin Boulders. He had ruled deceit and double-dealing out of his life and so he decided that he would frankly admit to Conners that he had endured the Yuma prison and had once been known as Hank Teed.

When face to face with Conners, he found his fears were groundless.

Tough and bluff Conners almost welcomed him with open arms. This was an era when numerous noted frontier trigger men became reformed – or at least so they claimed – and took up positions as lawmen. Their reputations added clout to the efforts of struggling marshals and sheriffs.

Twin Boulders was a raw, rip-roaring town, plagued by a spell of lawlessness and even the heavy-handed Lew Conners needed a deputy who could match his own rugged approach. He enthusiastically took Bob Young on, with the stipulation that he should resume the gun-slinging persona of Hank Teed and make no secret of formerly riding with the Alonzo Keller gang.

Hence, Young followed a spectacular course as the town's deputy who was dangerous if challenged by lawbreakers but a scrupulously honest public servant, well respected in the town.

A second letter from Dick revealed that he was to go to New Mexico to follow up a mystery that had occurred somewhere near a landmark known as Crouching Lion, close to the town of Blue Mesa.

The town, it seemed, was pretty well the personal fiefdom of a powerful cattleman named Walt Guisewell who, Dick heard, possessed a hard-as-nails reputation. He was, it seemed, one of the now dwindling band of old-time kings of the ranges who boasted that his word was law in his own dust-heap.

The details of this mission of Dick's were obviously

wrapped in secrecy. Dick never revealed anything of its nature and he had written that his own part in the mission was strictly an undercover one.

When he reached Blue Mesa, he wrote from the Mesa House to say he was moving around the region in the guise of a travelling artist.

Dick described Guisewell as a dominant personality, always menacingly in the background. His ranch crew were a ruffianly bunch but Dick made contact with them on their occasional visits to the saloon and, once or twice, played cards with them. In spite of their rough behaviour he found that he could tolerate them

He intimated in his note that, whatever his purpose in Blue Mesa was, he had to keep one jump ahead of Guisewell and his henchmen. There was no doubting the fact that he mistrusted the rancher and his hands.

A letter that proved to be his last one said that he had been making investigations near Crouching Lion, but did not explain what he was searching for.

Then, after a spell of silence, another letter for Bob Young arrived at the marshal's office in Twin Boulders.

It was from the detective agency employing Dick. It said Dick had gone missing while riding near Crouching Lion.

The company could never reveal what Dick's purpose was in travelling around New Mexico Territory. To do so would be to betray the trust of those who had commissioned its services. The company contacted Bob because Dick had given his name as next of kin and had detailed his whereabouts.

The agency put out feelers about the mystery surrounding Dick. It appeared that there had been no official investigation into his disappearance in Blue Mesa.

This information spurred Bob Young. Now with adequate savings behind him, he decided to quit the deputy's post and go to Blue Mesa to find out why Dick had vanished.

He was determined to push hard for positive results and to strive unyieldingly against any obstacle; he felt from the start that Walt Guisewell would prove to be obstructive.

He had no concrete evidence of the autocratic Guisewell being in any way responsible for his brother's disappearance, but Dick had written that the rancher cast a menacing shadow over Blue Mesa; there was a popular feeling that he and the unsavoury bunch he hired as hands were answerable for much dubious activity in the region.

From the outset Bob would make it known that he was on a determined mission; the weapon tied down to his thigh would be the seal guaranteeing its success.

He had established his credentials when he walked in on Guisewell's riders in the Lucky Dollar and showed his readiness to make trouble if provoked. Then his visit to the newspaper office in Sandy Crossing and what he learned there further shaped the direction of the business he had in hand.

Sprawled on his bed in the Mesa House he thought for a while, resisting the temptation to fall asleep, lulled by the drowsy heat. He returned the letters to his wallet and resolved to make the morrow a busy day.

Then he rose to call in on Cooty Sawkins at the Ace Café for a bite of supper.

CHAPTER EIGHT

QUESTIONS FOR THE MARSHAL

The sun was already blazing, the air humid and without the merest breath of a breeze when Bob Young stepped across the street the following morning. Again, the Ace Café contained only Cooty Sawkins and himself as he ate breakfast.

He wondered how Sawkins made a living since all the Blue Mesa residents seemed to prefer their own home catering to what the café offered, excellent though it was.

As usual, the café proprietor appeared guarded in his conversation and was markedly reluctant to go into much detail about Walt Guisewell. There was little doubt that the situation obtaining in the rancher's bailiwick kept Sawkins as well as Rube Cousins permanently timid if not actually scared.

Bob deliberately avoided the subject of Guisewell and the hold he had on the town, but he quietly monitored the effect of living in Blue Mesa's atmosphere had on both

Sawkins and Cousins. Someday he would coax information out of them.

After breakfast he walked along the boardwalk to the office of the city marshal into which he had seen the little W Bar G hand scoot after his arrival in town.

The sun-warped board building had a woebegone look and displayed little pride in the town's policing arm. The shingle over the door read: TOWN MARSHAL: EZRA TODD.

Young shoved the door open and entered a cramped, airless, office. There were the barred doors to a couple of cells to one side. The room held a pair of battered filing cabinets, a small table littered with documents and a large desk in one corner. In the sweaty, stifling heat the place hardly suggested energetic activity; it looked ramshackle in the extreme.

An obese, middle-aged man sat behind the desk. He wore a marshal's star on his vest. In keeping with his surroundings, he did not look like one who would spring into lively action.

Beside the desk stood a tall, slightly stooped man who sported the smaller badge of a deputy on his grimy shirt. He had a tired appearance and looked as if he had put his best years behind him.

This was the first Young had seen of the full complement of Blue Mesa's force for the maintenance of law, for he had never witnessed either the city marshal or his deputy patrolling the street.

Both lawmen started as Young stepped in and the eyes of each registered surprise, even near alarm. Young reflected that his fame had been carried ahead of him by the W Bar G rider he had seen hastening into the office after his arrival at the Lucky Dollar.

'Marshal Todd?' he asked.

'Yes, I'm Todd,' said the fat man behind the desk. His voice was husky and apprehensive.

'I'm Bob Young and I want to ask questions.'

'About what?' The marshal's eyes seemed fixed on the tied-down holster.

The deputy had also spotted it and Young noted how the man took a step back when he approached the desk, as if the newcomer were carrying a contagious disease.

'About a man named Young and a couple of unknown men who vanished near Crouching Lion, and why you, as the nearest law officer, did not mount an inquiry when you had word of these incidents. I figure you *did* hear about them. Into the bargain, what happened to their horses?'

Todd looked scared, nevertheless he showed he was game for some verbal fencing with Young.

'None of that concerns me,' he said. 'All that's for the county sheriff and I'm only marshal of Blue Mesa. It all happened off my jurisdiction.'

'Don't lecture me on peacekeeping procedure, Marshal. If you had word of these matters and you truly were the nearest peace officer, it was your duty to tell the county sheriff everything you knew. I believe you didn't do it. If you had, any dutiful sheriff would have pushed for some deep investigations.'

He was playing a wild card here, trusting that the information given to him by Mike Fraser was accurate: he had the gut feeling that the editor's word could indeed be trusted.

He stepped a pace nearer the desk, causing the thin deputy to jump back yet again.

He placed both hands on the desk and leaned forward, staring Ezra Todd square in the face. Todd's eyes widened and he began to shift uncomfortably. A larger blob of perspiration ran down his already sweaty face.

'I'll tell you what I think, Marshal. I think you're a damned poor specimen as an officer of the law,' Young growled slowly. 'I'm sure you heard of these missing men but you didn't follow the book. And I'm plumb sure that was because Walt Guisewell ordered it.'

He suddenly dropped his hand to his low-slung holster, causing the marshal and his deputy to jump. He rested his hand on the butt of his gun. He softened his abrasive tone and became almost conversational saying, 'You know, gentlemen, it is unfortunate that Mr Guisewell has such a hold on this country that he figures he can control it just as he pleases. He might consider himself to be a sort of benevolent spirit – he could even think that the people of this town have an unbounded love and respect for him. Now that's where he gets it most awfully wrong.'

He paused, put on a mournful expression and continued, 'Unhappily, I heard whispers to the contrary. It seems there are some in Blue Mesa who hanker after taking up arms against him; the place could explode under his very feet like a powder keg.' He shook his head despairingly.

'I'd sure feel sorry for any men who tried to keep the peace in a town that had blown itself all to hell in that way. And I have a feeling these mysterious incidents at Crouching Lion could bring that kind of situation about.'

'I swear I know nothing about it,' gasped Todd in a squeaky voice. 'Nothing concerning any incidents at Crouching Lion was ever reported here.'

The skinny, stooped deputy found a voice, as jittery as Todd's.

'Marshal Todd's telling the truth,' he bleated. Young fixed them with a hard glare.

'I know you are both lying but I reckon it's a fair wager that the man who seems to know just about everything worth knowing in this region can tell me something about the affair: I mean Mr Walt Guisewell,' said Young deliberately.

The two lawmen looked at him almost astonished. It was as if he had committed some unspeakable breach of proper behaviour by bringing the rancher's name into it. They appeared to venerate Guisewell as the be-all and end-all of their existence, but then his coffers were deep and he paid big wages to those who jumped to his word.

Young straightened up and considered them, one sitting and the other standing and both looking paralysed with apprehension. With a quirky grin but with his eyes reflecting no humour, he said:

'I'm in a mood to go prodding around powerful hard for answers. So I guess I'll bide my time until I eventually discover how Mr Guisewell himself responds to some prodding.'

He turned and made for the door, leaving the pair still appearing paralysed and aghast.

He crossed the street and headed for the Mesa House.

Except for lunch and supper at the Ace Café, where yet again he was the solitary customer, he spent the rest of the day in his room, sweating out the increasingly oppressive heat, thinking deeply and forming a plan of action.

While Young was at lunch Horace Slack, deputy to

Marshal Ezra Todd, slipped quietly out of the rear of the town marshal's office to the stable behind the building, saddled his horse and rode hastily out of town. He took the southern trail, the direct route to Guisewell's ranch. He pushed the horse to a speed which, in such sweltering weather, punished the animal. After the briefest of rests at the Split Rock Sink, where both rider and mount drank, he resumed the saddle and set a smart lick for the W Bar G.

Slack was almost as lathered as his horse as he rode through the great arch of peeled poles into the ranch yard.

Walt Guisewell saw his arrival from the gallery. He went down to the yard and was waiting in the path of the animal as Slack pulled rein and brought it to a slithering halt.

Several of the hands in various parts of the yard witnessed the coming of the deputy and ambled over to stand alongside the rancher.

Guisewell had little regard for the deputy law officer of Blue Mesa, whom he considered to be among the least of his hirelings.

'Why all the blasted hurry?' he hooted.

'That Bob Young is stirring up trouble! He came into our office and claimed you know something about … well … you know … the doings at Crouching Lion,' panted Slack, finally spluttering out the reference to a subject he did not want to speak of.

'Oh, he did, did he?' grunted Guisewell, visibly startled.

Horace Slack delivered a colourfully garbled version of what Young had said in the office.

'He admitted he was making trouble in the town, Mr Guisewell. Said he was getting people to take up arms against you and set the place off like a powder keg under your feet.'

'He said that, did he?' snorted the rancher. 'By God, I always suspected that most of the damned ungrateful population of that blamed town never appreciated how well I treated them. And if Young wants powder kegs to go off, I'll give him and Blue Mesa explosions aplenty!'

'He sounded … real … determined, Mr Guisewell,' Slack said in his breathless, dithering way. Guisewell spat into the dust.

'Well, I'm a damned sight more determined than he is. You skedaddle back to Blue Mesa, Slack, and you and Todd get ready for trouble coming on the hoof. And, when the shooting starts, take good care you don't shoot at me and the boys. You shoot at what we shoot at. Understood?'

'Understood,' affirmed Slack half-heartedly and with a gulp. He turned his horse around and headed back to town.

Guisewell turned to the audience of hard-bitten wranglers with a face of thunder.

'I told you jokers to have your shooting irons ready,' he growled. 'Well, get yourselves well equipped with ammunition. There's a wild time coming up!'

Back in Blue Mesa, Bob Young was again sprawling on his bed, thinking about his exploits that day. He was sure word of his visit to the two lawmen would be relayed to Walt Guisewell.

Just as night fell he looked at the street from his window. It was deserted and deadly quiet but it retained the same brooding threat of lurking trouble that had hit him when he first rode into it.

He reasoned that there must almost certainly be a combustible stock of animosity building up against him in Blue

Mesa and its locality and just as certainly he would have added fuel to it with his visit to the lawmen.

Some violent reaction might explode around him when he was least prepared for it.

That night, he slid his Colt from its tied-down holster and slept with it, fully loaded, under his pillow.

By the time he fell into an uneasy sleep he had formed a firm resolution for the morrow.

CHAPTER NINE

YOUNG PAYS A VISIT

In the morning Bob Young came down the stairs to make for the Ace Café and breakfast. In the lobby he met Rube Cousins

'Rube, suppose a fellow wanted to visit the W Bar G, which direction would he take from here?' he asked casually. Cousins looked at him with rounded eyes, then he frowned.

'You don't mean you aim to go there?' he gasped.

'Well, why not?' said Young light-heartedly. 'It might be a pleasant ride on a bright morning like this.'

The old-timer gulped. 'You'd be pushing your luck if you go into Guisewell's den. Nobody can prove anything, but there are suspicions that he was behind your brother's disappearance, just as there have been a heap of goings-on in this country over the years that Guisewell was surely responsible for.'

'Well, pushing my luck is what I came here for; to push and prod until I get at the reason why Dick vanished, as well as another couple of fellows I now know about. And I mean to prod real hard, Rube.' He slapped his Colt meaningfully. Rube Cousins frowned.

'You could be putting yourself into a nest of rattlers.'

'Well, if I don't show up back in town by tomorrow morning, I'd be obliged if I could look to you for a favour. I take it there's no telegraph office in Blue Mesa?'

'You bet there isn't,' said Cousins. 'That's not the kind of link with civilization that would suit Guisewell.'

'I guess there's one in Sandy Crossing, so if I show up missing you – or someone trustworthy – go over to Sandy Crossing and telegraph the US marshal in Las Cruces and ask him to come to Blue Mesa. Give him the note that's under the mattress on my bed. Mike Fraser, the editor of the paper in Sandy Crossing, will prove a good friend if you need one.'

'I'll do everything you say, Mr Young. I'll see to it myself,' said Cousins suddenly looking surprisingly sprightly.

He proceeded to instruct Young on the way to reach the W Bar G headquarters by way of the Split Rock Sink, after which, said Cousins, he would find a signpost showing the way to the ranch.

Young breakfasted at the Ace Café and, after the meal, made deliberate preparations for a ride under a sun already showing signs of rising to another merciless zenith.

In the hotel stable he brushed down his horse to rid it of the accumulated dust of travel, fed and watered it, then checked the chambers of his Colt. He took his Winchester carbine from its saddle scabbard, checked its magazine, then performed the unusual action of pumping the weapon to cock it before returning it to its scabbard,

After taking leave of Rube Cousins, he rode off, leaving

Cousins watching his departing back, shaking his head and muttering to himself, 'Can't think what he hopes to do. He talks of prodding. I just hope he don't prod himself into his grave.'

Young rode at an easy pace, struck the Split Rock Sink, where he took the break for refreshment usual for those en route to the W Bar G and, after passing the fingerpost showing the way to the ranch, quickened his pace a little.

He passed through the arched gateway into the ranch yard and found a scene of bustling activity there. In the centre of the yard there was a large corral in which ranch hands were busy amidst a cluster of bawling and shifting steers. Smoke circled over the heads of the men and the still air carried the reek of burning hides. He had arrived in the middle of a branding session.

Several hands watched his approach and drifted away from their tasks to stand against the poles of the corral and gaze at him inquisitively

Scrawny Slim Forster, who remembered Young as Hank Teed from his Wyoming days, was standing outside the corral. He saw Young approaching and he quickly scooted out of the way to shelter behind the big harness shed close to the corral, where he stayed hidden. He had vivid memories of this man with the tied-down holster wreaking six-gun havoc in his earlier career.

Forster sensed that Young could only have intruded into the W Bar G to deliver a package of trouble.

Walt Guisewell looked up from the midst of a branding party, saw Young and made his way to the corral fence. Surprisingly lithe for one no longer young, he quickly climbed the poles and dropped down to the other side.

This was the first time he ever laid eyes on Young but

there was no mistaking this newcomer's identity – or the meaning of his tied-down holster.

As Young halted his horse the rancher walked forward briskly to stand in front of the man and his mount.

'You're Young,' he hooted. 'What the hell are you doing on my property?'

'Visiting, Mr Guisewell. Visiting, to pay you a call and to prod you a little by way of telling you I have a notion you know something about why my brother and two more men disappeared. More than likely they're all dead and I reckon you can answer for their deaths.'

'You've got a damned nerve, coming in here and making allegations,' exploded Guisewell.

'Yes, I figure some prodding will make you answer to the law,' said Young evenly, as if he had not heard the rancher. 'And I don't mean the so-called law you established in Blue Mesa to be served up by Todd and Slack. No, sir, I mean the genuine, rock-solid law of the United States.'

Guisewell's face darkened with anger and his eyes showed malignant intention as he made a determined snatching move towards his holstered pistol.

At once, with eye-defying speed, Young grabbed for his Colt: the weapon was in his hand and pointing unwaveringly at the rancher before Guisewell could clutch the butt of his gun.

'Don't attempt it,' commanded Young. 'Once that gun is in your hand, your prize crew of saddle-bums will be mourning their boss.' His eyes swept over the array of cowhands lining the further side of the corral fence while, at the same time, seeming to keep Guisewell under their gaze.

Pete Hazen, some little way along the line at Guisewell's

back, made a reckless move towards the holster at his belt. Young responded with a surprising action.

With the muzzle of his Colt still directed at Walt Guisewell, he dipped his body to the left, quickly reached down towards his saddle-scabbard and, again with uncanny rapidity, came up with his already cocked Winchester carbine.

Hazen, with his gun still undrawn, stood frozen and open-mouthed as he found himself covered by the mouth of the carbine, the stock of which Young had almost miraculously contrived to grip under his upper left arm. His right hand still steadily pointed the Colt at Guisewell.

'This carbine's already cocked, Hazen,' Young assured the foreman. 'Any smart moves from either of you will bring on a quick attack of lead poisoning.'

The lined-up hands stood just as frozen to the spot as was Hazen. They watched Young, who still kept the rancher and his foreman covered by two weapons in his novel fashion. He addressed Guisewell loudly and clearly

'The reason I rode out here, Mr Guisewell, is because I don't care to fight a man without giving him some idea of the odds against him – and, believe me, I *am* fighting you. The odds against you are those same rock-solid federal laws which I aim to throw in your face – if I find sufficient evidence for doing so. Maybe I'll never find the evidence, so you'll have nothing to fear but, depend on it, I'm hard on your tail, looking for the evidence.'

He paused and looked along the line of Guisewell's henchmen with open disdain, still keeping the rancher and his foreman under the muzzles of his two weapons.

'So there are my cards on the table and I've delivered the message I came to deliver,' he told them. 'Now, I'll turn around and ride off. Don't any of you think of shooting me in the back, because for all you know the forces of US law are already primed to look into the affairs of the Guisewell kingdom.'

He made a quick, unerring display of jamming his Colt into its holster, releasing his carbine from its under-arm security, and, spinning it round by the trigger guard, dropped it neatly into the scabbard below his left knee..

Just as neatly he danced his horse around and rode slowly towards the great arches of the yard gate, presenting his back to the W Bar G men as though in disdain.

On the inner side of the corral rail the hands turned their sun-punished and whisker-fringed faces towards Guisewell. He was glowering at the retreating back of Young and he was visibly shaking. All his bluster was spent. He had been scared by the prospect of the law of the land being invoked to override the rickety and crooked law he had established in the roost he ruled.

Bob Young had thoroughly humiliated him in the company of his hirelings. Pete Hazen, who was closest to the rancher, spoke in a half whisper:

'We can fix him right now, before he rides off W Bar G land, Mr Guisewell.'

'No!' commanded Guisewell sharply. 'Not in the back.'

Hazen's inner reaction was to think that this was a strangely ethical retort to come from Guisewell. He remembered the bushwhacking forays he and the others had been sent on by the rancher while Guisewell himself stayed home at the W Bar G.

There had been those long periods of lying in wait among the rocks near Crouching Lion until their victims rode up. Much later there had been a repeat performance to drop Dick Young into the dust after they found out that he was investigating the vanishing of the pair. There had been no prissy objections to back-shooting on those occasions.

'I've got my plans made,' growled Guisewell. 'I've got everything good and ready.'

All the W Bar G men had heard this sort of talk from their boss before. Now they wondered when he was going to start his fight.

Bob Young, with a few backward glances to reassure himelf that he was not being followed, rode clear of the W Bar G lands.

CHAPTER TEN

THE MAN IN THE ALLEY

The brilliant sun of the following morning warned Young of the man lurking in the alley beside the Mesa House.

He had stepped out of the hotel to go and breakfast at the café when he noticed that the sun's rays, shining directly down the alley, were casting on to the ground at its entrance the distinct shadow of a figure in a sombrero. Clearly, the man must be very close to this end of the alley.

Young drew his gun with lightning swiftness, took half a dozen noiseless paces along the boardwalk, and slipped quickly around the corner of the alley with his weapon pointing at the startled man he found only a yard in front of him. Just behind him was a saddled horse laden with a bedroll and a bulky war sack – the trappings of a man who was travelling.

The lurker in the alley was a tall, stick-thin man in range garb. He had the kind of slack-jawed face that might give the impression that he was a dullard.

As soon as Young appeared with his naked Colt, the

lurker's hands shot up in surrender and Young recognized him as one of the W Bar G crew whom he'd seen at the saloon and again at the W Bar G headquarters.

'Don't shoot, Mr Young,' the ranny said in a slow drawl. 'I was waiting here to see you. Didn't want to stand out on the street. Too blamed conspicuous and too near the office of that no-account Marshal Todd and his dimwit of a deputy, Horace Slack. Been here since soon after sunup.'

'You're one of Guisewell's men,' said Young accusingly.

'I was but I ain't now. I quit last night. Sneaked off when everyone in the bunkhouse was asleep, loaded up my gear and vamoosed. I walked out on Guisewell, even though he owes me for half a month's work.'

Young, remembering his precautions of the night, looked about him quickly. Was this a ruse? Had he unwittingly walked into a trap? He saw no sign of anyone else in the alley and lowered his weapon.

'Name's Cal Davis,' continued the man. 'I drifted out of Texas a couple of months ago and Guisewell took me on to his payroll. I'll admit I was never an angel. I was in the Confederate Army, saw some ugly things in the war and did some ugly things, but there comes a time when a man has to think about straightening out his life.'

'I understand that.' Young nodded as he returned his gun to its holster.

'In no time, I saw the W Bar G was no place for me,' Davis went on bitterly. 'Guisewell pays top money, sure, but he expects a man to crawl to him like he was some kind of blasted king. He figures he can buy a man, heart and soul. I couldn't take to that and I couldn't take to the gang riding for him.

'A good few are certainly on the dodge. They were full of

74

secrets, kind of whispered among themselves. A couple of times I heard mention of bushwhackings near Crouching Lion and I got the notion some of them were in on it.'

Young raised an eyebrow. 'Did you learn who was involved?'

'No, but I suspect Pete Hazen was one and a joker named Forster was another. Both would ride to hell on Guisewell's say-so.

'You showed up and some claimed you were here to make trouble because of your brother's disappearance. I said that from the little I knew about the bushwhacking you couldn't be blamed for feeling good and sore. I was told to shut up and I've been cold-shouldered ever since.'

'I'm obliged to you for your sentiments.' said Young. 'Did you hear anything more about the bushwhacking antics?'

'Only one little thing, which I couldn't figure out. I once overheard Hazen mention to Forster that there was some sort of evidence at Crouching Lion that Guisewell wished he could get rid of.'

'Evidence? Now, that's a loaded word,' murmured Young. 'It makes Guisewell sound guilty.'

'Oh, he's plenty guilty,' said Davis. 'Anyway, I was hanging around here to warn you.'

'To warn me?'

'Yes, about trouble coming up. First off, Guisewell saw the piece you put in the Sandy Crossing paper, and that sent him into a hell of a fury. He yelled at the whole crew to get ready for a showdown with you. It's something he's been growling about since you hit town.'

Young listened intently with a growing conviction that he could trust this deserter from the W Bar G camp. Davis went on, 'Then, Horace Slack, Marshal Ezra Todd's dumb deputy, rode into the W Bar G, shouting about you going into their office and making threats. That got Guisewell's dander up even worse.'

'Good.' Young grinned. 'I get a great deal of pleasure out of making Walt Guisewell uncomfortable.'

'Then, you showed up just when I was good and tired of Guisewell's war talk and you caused me to think of cutting loose from him and his outfit. He's been fixing to settle your hash. Now, he reckons he's about to do it pretty damned quick.

'At the same time, he's kind of scared of you. You made reference to United States law and it's plain he and some others have the idea you're in with the federal lawmen. But US law or not, he's just about half-cracked enough to charge at you bull-headed and be damned to the consequences.'

Davis paused, then added, 'He says he'll get you if it means shooting up all of Blue Mesa and he's mad at the town because, according to Slack, you said it's ready to go off like a powder keg in rebellion against him.'

Young gave his quirky grin. 'Well, let's hope he does it after I've had some breakfast.' He jerked his head towards the Ace Café, feeling he owed Cal Davis a token of gratitude. 'Care for a bite to eat?'

'No, thanks, I'll shake the dust of this damned town off my boots and head for the Texas line. I heard of an outfit hiring down near El Paso.' Davis turned and moved towards his laden horse.

'Then thanks again and good luck,' said Young. He strode off in the direction of Cooty Sawkins's eating house.

He crossed the street with his mind on what he had just heard from Cal Davis. The indications were that Walt

Guisewell was all set to bring on his fight. Would his crew of hardcases follow him to a man? Would he bring them storming into Blue Mesa like a vengeful army to kill Young even if it meant shooting up the town?

What would be the reaction of the rest of the townsmen, the traders and merchants who struggled to flourish in an environment with an unfriendly reputation? What of all the little folk who lay low and endured the rancher's grip on their liberty?

One consideration on Young's mind was the personal fate of Guisewell. If he should come into Blue Mesa shooting, Young did not want him to be killed. He had warned the rancher that he was out to fight him with the due process of United States law; he hoped to see Guisewell alive, tried and, provided enough sound evidence against him was discovered, convicted in court.,

As usual, the Ace Café was empty of other customers when Young walked in. Cooty Sawkins, who always kept up a bright front, offered him a cheerful greeting as Young seated himself at his usual table and called for his usual breakfast. While Cooty was serving him he asked, 'Tell me, Cooty, would you bear arms against Walt Guisewell if he and his outfit rode into town to make trouble – I mean real, hot-lead trouble?'

Sawkins looked at him with suspicion. 'If you mean in a case of whether it was either me or him and his crew who survived, I'd be fighting for me. Sure I'd bear arms. Guisewell never did me any favours. He's put such a jinx on this town I've been within a mule's kick of bankruptcy for years. Folks avoid Blue Mesa and every last one of us business people needs customers.'

Young smiled at Cooty's unexpectedly spirited display

of nerve.

'I always took you for a timid soul, Cooty,' he said.

'Timid be damned!' growled Cooty. 'I have a Winchester back in my quarters and it sure won't act timid if called upon. Yes, I'd fight to get out from under Guisewell's boot heel. If this town could breathe easier it would be all the better for folks like Rube Cousins at the hotel and me. We've been sweating to keep failing businesses alive for years.'

'Where would Rube stand if there was a showdown? I'd figured him for being kind of timid also.'

'Don't you believe it,' said Cooty with a sharp laugh. 'He's got more fire in his belly than me but he keeps it damped down. There's nothing else a man can do when he's put every last cent into a venture only to be bulldogged by the like of Walt Guisewell and his bunch of hardcases calling the tune and laying down the law.'

Cooty paused, looked at Young with raised eyebrows and, dropping his voice almost to a whisper, asked with some eagerness:

'Why are we talking on this subject? Are you planning something?'

'No, but trouble could come. Guisewell's making war-talk and it seems it's more than bluster.'

'Well, I'm ready for it,' declared Cooty, sticking his chin out belligerently. 'I have no wife, no kids and nothing to lose except a business that could be a good one but is only just limping along. Yes, by thunder, I'm ready for a fight!'

Young left the café smiling slightly at the thought of little Cooty in the role of a fighting man, but he was fully convinced of the café-owner's determination.

As he crossed the street he saw three men standing by

the steps of the Mesa House. Three horses were hitched to the hotel's rack.

The men had the look of solid citizens and were dressed in sober but not expensive-looking outfits. Young noted that each wore a shell belt at his waist and their holsters sported either a Colt or a Smith & Wesson revolver.

Approaching them, he tried to size up who they might be. Each was nearing middle age and the look of the whole trio suggested experience of the storms of life. He conjectured that each had probably served on one side or the other in the Civil War.

One man, lean, muscular and with a sandy beard, stepped forward to meet him.

'Mr Young?'

'Yes.'

The stranger stretched out a hand. 'We're from over Sandy Crossing way. I'm Sam Willows and these gents are Harry Cornford and Karl Hessell. We were once settled in this town, though settled ain't the right word. We all rented premises from Walt Guisewell and tried to run businesses, Harry and Karl in a dry-goods partnership and me as a harness maker.'

Young shook the proffered hand and Willows went on, 'One way and another, we put up with a lot of harassment from Guisewell, who took the line that we had put ourselves under his thumb just by being in his town.'

The man whom Sam Willows had identified as Karl Hessell added, 'What Sam means is that he seemed to figure he could order us around like we were his hired hands instead of being independent traders, paying him rent.'

'And paying it regularly, according to agreement,' put

in Harry Cornford. Young gave a sardonic chuckle.

'From what I know of him, that's Guisewell's way. Seems he can't help kicking everyone around.'

'We got plumb sick of it and all three of us decided to quit Blue Mesa and set up afresh in Sandy Crossing,' explained Sam Willows. 'That notice you put in our newspaper brought us back here, otherwise we'd keep well clear of the damned place. Karl here has something to tell you. Cough it up, Karl.'

'Well, some time before those shootings at Crouching Lion,' said Hessell, 'I was riding the trail out of Sandy Crossing to deliver some goods to a customer. Coming up to where the trail forks, one way leading to Crouching Lion, I saw a bunch of riders heading towards me. There was something familiar about them, something I didn't like.'

'Guisewell's men?' asked Young. Hessel nodded.

'Even at a distance I figured I knew some of them. It seems they did not spot me and I headed my cayuse into some rocks and watched. I saw them take the trail to Crouching Lion and I thought it was odd that they should be so far away from the bulk of the W Bar G holdings, though I knew Guisewell claimed his lands spread out that way.'

'Could you identify any of them?'

'Well, Pete Hazen was in the lead for sure. There's no mistaking his fat figure, and I believe I recognized Forster. Well, pretty soon after that tales began to fly around Sandy Crossing that a couple of strangers had hired horses in town. They had headed for Crouching Lion but were never seen again. Then we heard that the artist Dick Young, who'd been seen around town, had also disappeared somewhere near Crouching Lion.'

'We three got to talking about these things one night when we met up,' put in Harry Cornford. 'Karl remembered how he saw the W Bar G bunch riding in the direction of Crouching Lion right around the time in question. None of us is ever likely to think anything good of Guisewell and his crew: we figure Karl saw Hazen and the rest on their way to make trouble.'

'You could be right. There's a chance of trouble from Guisewell right here in his own bailiwick at any minute.'

'Seems you're fit to meet trouble at any time,' said Willows, nodding pointedly towards the tied-down holster.

'I might have no choice since Guisewell is personally out to kill me; he claims he'll do it even if it means shooting up his whole town. Maybe that's all a windy boast but he and his bunch might on their way right now.'

All three men from Sandy Crossing raised their eyebrows at that and looked at Young more intently. Each now appeared less like a tradesman, more like a seasoned campaigner, as if signs of his experiences in the Civil War were becoming evident.

'Seems you could use some support,' said Harry Cornford, slapping the Smith & Wesson at his waist.

'Could be,' responded Young casually.

'Harry's got a point there,' said Sam Willows. 'I figure the three of us should take time out for coffee in the café yonder and discuss where we stand on the matter.'

'Good idea,' approved Young. 'Cooty Sawkins will be right glad of your custom and if you find him oiling up his Winchester it's because he already knows where he stands. I'm about to look in on Rube Cousins at the hotel here to ask about his intentions.'

'You mean there could be a united front of the townsfolk

against Guisewell?' asked Karl Hessell, who appeared eager for a fight.

'Possibly. It all depends on the way most folks feel about Guisewell.'

Young watched the trio walk off towards the Ace Café; middle-aged men with developing paunches who suddenly had the look of youths in blue or grey, marching towards the gunfire at Shiloh or Gettysburg.

He found Rube Cousins standing in the lobby of the hotel. Cousins's curiosity had been aroused earlier when he observed Young in conversation with the three men from Sandy Crossing.

'Those three were traders here in Blue Mesa,' Cousins commented. 'They had the good sense to get out from under Guisewell's thumb. They're good men.'

'So they seem,' said Young. 'How do *you* feel about getting out from under?'

Cousins looked at him with a decidedly pugnacious expression. 'In favour. Pretty damned keenly in favour!'

Young laughed. 'You know, I'd pegged you and Cooty Sawkins as kind of timid but I discovered Cooty is a fighting man underneath the surface.'

'Me, too. Cooty and me might act timid because Guisewell forced us into a hole long ago and we were both dispirited. I assure you a heap of defiance is corked up in both of us and it's just hankering to bust out. Guisewell has pushed us and others around and he's used his damned gunhawks to intimidate folks in this town.'

'You might have a chance to let it loose before long.'

'I know it. There are rumours flying around town, spread by that fool deputy Horace Slack. He claims he was at Guisewell's place and Guisewell is spitting fire, roaring

82

that he'll kill you if it means shooting up all Blue Mesa.'

'Is anyone else likely to resist if Guisewell brings on a fight?'

'Oh, sure. More than you know. Tom Gross, the blacksmith; Jack Cummins, the lumber merchant; Lafe McCracken, the carpenter and undertaker – though he'll probably be accused of getting involved so as to stack up the body count for business purposes. I know the under-currents of feeling in Blue Mesa. Walt Guisewell thinks he has the place in his fist but he's badly mistaken.' Cousins grinned and, self-mockingly, came to attention like a soldier. 'Then there's me, a powerful force to be reckoned with, Mr Young,' he declared. 'I was there when the bugle sounded in eighteen sixty-one and, old as I am, I'm still fit for battle.'

'Listen,' said Young with grave emphasis, 'if we're in for a big fight with Guisewll and his outfit, get the word around the townspeople not to aim at Guisewell. I want him alive so he can be brought before the law if a case can be made against him.'

'That's a tall order,' grunted Cousins. 'A good number of folks would like to see him paid out in the way of the old West, but I reckon Cooty and I can spread the message around those who're eager for action.'

Young walked out of the hotel wearing a look of satisfac-tion but aware that he was itching under a sudden curious urge that he could not explain.

So, tensions rose under the surface of Blue Mesa. The town wondered whether some bloody, bullet-riddled upheaval was about to come upon it, or was the apparent threat of trouble no more than furious bluster by Walt Guisewell.

Rumours flew; the visitors from Sandy Crossing mulled over the question of their taking part in any trouble; Cooty Sawkins looked to his armaments while Rube Cousins shed his pacific demeanour and rediscovered his old martial spirit.

Only minutes after leaving the Mesa House and in the face of this uneasy apprehension, Bob Young, the man with the tied-down holster who had shown up out of the blue with the swagger of a gunslinger to set this whole state of affairs in motion, did something quite unexpected.

He rode out of town.

He knew that he did so only because he was thrust into it by a seemingly illogical urge that he could not explain.

Young rode in the direction of Crouching Lion. He could not explain why he was seized by the notion to investigate that location just at the time when a dark and brooding anticipation of impending crisis was gripping the township of Blue Mesa.

He saw that he, who was central to the creation of the crisis, could be accused of skipping town just when his trigger skills were about to be required.

In an understandably frank evaluation of his behaviour some townsfolk might hold that he had simply turned yellow.

Later he wondered if, however illogical it might seem, his journeying to Crouching Lion might be because he was impelled to respond to a call from that unknown time and place beyond the curtain of the centuries separating the dwellers in an earlier era from those of his own day.

Perhaps in some way a psychic link had been established between himself and the cultural world represented by the legends surrounding Crouching Lion, and it was snatching him away from the imminent urgent affairs at Blue Mesa.

As his horse got into its stride the late-morning sun was reaching its zenith and threatening an even fiercer intensity than in previous days. From the Sangre de Cristo Mountains in the north to the Sierra Guadalupe in the south, it blasted its heat down on New Mexico Territory.

These were conditions that caused the greybeards to mop their brows and prophesy that the weather must surely break in bellowing thunderstorms and torrential rain or the whole world would be burned to a crisp.

Young approached Crouching Lion, though he was not wholly sure that he was taking the wisest course.

He was highly intrigued by the story told by Cal Davis that there was evidence at Crouching Lion that Walt Guisewell wanted to destroy. Anything that led to clarifying the fate of the men who had disappeared was apt to take priority in the mind of Bob Young.

Was this the right time to seek out whatever evidence he might find at Crouching Lion?

Young hoped Guisewell's threatened showdown at Blue Mesa did not occur while he was busying himself at the place of the naturally sculpted Crouching Lion.

He allowed his mount to plod the dusty trail at a leisurely pace, sparing its energy in the blaze of midday. There was a halt for man and animal to drink at a minor stream where the water was ominously low. He hit the Crouching Lion location near noon.

Without quite knowing what he was searching for he left his horse on the trail under the shadow of the giant natural sculpture and walked the trail, looking at the harsh, sandy land. On his left hand was the rising wall of tumbled boulders and caves, which could give perfect cover to any assassin intent on shooting a rider on the trail below.

Abruptly, he came upon several distinct marks scored into the surface of the trail. They continued over a tract of land clear of rocks and on up a slight rise to the mouth of a cave, which was the most significant feature of the sheer rock wall.

Plainly, some object – or possibly more than one – had been dragged or shoved along the ground up to and into the cave.

Young trudged up the rise and entered the gloom of the cave.

He was at once aware of the odour hanging in the broiling atmosphere. It was the highly unpleasant stench of decayed flesh. He screwed his eyes against the poor light and saw the cause of the odour visible in the gloom towards the rear of the cave.

Humped there were three near-skeletons of horses, all bearing clinging remnants of the last vestiges of rotted flesh.

To add to the ominous atmosphere, some creature, seen only as a fleeting streak, scuttled rapidly away from the vicinity of the skeletons and into the total darkness of the deepest portion of the cave.

Young considered the disposition of the animal remains. Two were close to each other; the third and least badly decayed was some little distance from them, nearer the cave entrance. The rocky and sandy floor still bore tracks indicating that the dead animals had been dragged in from outside, doubtless at the expense of much sweat and energy.

It could easily be conjectured that the two animals dumped close to each other had been the mounts of the two strangers who disappeared before Dick Young arrived on the scene, and that the isolated one was what remained of Dick's horse, pulled in later after his killing.

Holding his nose, Young walked towards the two rotting carcasses lying close to each other. A portion of flesh and hide remained on one of the pair and, in the uncertain light, two branded letters on the hide could be made out: a K and a J. He examined a portion of the hide on the second carcass and found a similar brand of the same letters.

If these remains were those of the horses ridden by the two unknown travellers, the brand must be that of the livery stable in Sandy Crossing that had hired them out.

Nowhere to be seen were saddles, leather trappings or saddle baggage. Quite likely all had been pitched into the deep Crouching Lion chasm. Probably more than one man would have been required to haul the dead horses into the cave, and maybe the bodies of the two unknown men and Dick had either been secretly buried or also thrown into the chasm.

He stood in the sweltering, malodourous dimness of the cave, pondering the blotting out of the three lives. He was absolutely sure the whole grisly affair was the work of the W Bar G riders, seen by Karl Hessell. They must have spent quite some time in this region, staked out at an ambush site on two different occasions: first awaiting the two strangers, then lying in wait for Dick Young. But what was the reason behind the three killings?

Possibly it could be to scare others away: others who might be showing too much interest in Crouching Lion and its chasm. When questions about the vanished men were asked, the possibility of skulduggery by dangerous border ruffians could be trotted out.

But Bob Young knew that there was a deeper reason underlying this complicated riddle: something that involved Walt Guisewell up to the hilt.

CHAPTER ELEVEN

AT CROUCHING LION

Young tramped out of the cave and was grateful to be breathing clean air, heat-charged though it was. He felt that he now understood the sequence of dramatic events at Crouching Lion; like a sudden bright light it had dawned on him that the remains of the three horses in the cave constituted the evidence he guessed Guisewell wished to be rid of.

He recalled the outcroppings and shelves of rock he had seen jutting from the sides of the chasm. It might have been easy enough to throw the corpses of Dick Young and the two men who had also disappeared a sufficient distance into the air above the chasm to ensure that they fell cleanly to the bottom, but the bulky bodies of horses would have been a different matter.

They would have to be hauled to the lip and pushed over. Almost certainly, they would fall on to a ledge and remain there as incriminating evidence. So their slayers had hauled them into the cave, hoping they might be mere skeletons before they were found.

Deep in thought, Young walked down the slight rise, then stopped in his tracks. Standing right in front of him was the Apache whom he had glimpsed on his first visit. He was standing stock still, holding his lean body erect, suggesting that he did not intend to let Young pass.

He held up his right hand in a gesture of peace. Young saw that, despite his lithe body and erect bearing, his face was seamed by the years and he was much older than he had appeared from a distance. There was dignity and wisdom in his countenance.

The Apache pointed across the trail to the cave that Young had just left. He held up two fingers.

'Two times you come here. You officer? White man's law?' he asked in a deep, rumbling voice.

'Yes.' Young nodded. It might not be absolutely true but he had recently been a deputy marshal and he had come to examine the area of Crouching Lion wholly in the interests of justice.

The Apache held up three fingers and jerked his head towards the cave.

'Three horses yonder.' With his thumb he indicated the yawning chasm behind his back. 'Three *hombres – blancos –* white men. Corpses. Below in chasm.'

The significance of what the Indian was saying became vividly clear, shocking Young and filling him with a surge of emotion. It vindicated his conjectures about the brutal fate of Dick and two men who had also vanished. He gathered his wits and asked:

'And saddles and trappings were thrown into the chasm with the corpses, but the horses were too big to be treated that way, so they were dragged into the cave?'

'*Si* – yes,' responded the Apache, employing the mingling of Spanish and English common among his people, who had existed for generations throughout a vast region not named Mexico and the United States until late-coming invaders arrived from Europe.

'Did you see this happen?' Young asked.

'*Si*, all of it. Lone Apache keep well out of way of armed group of white men today. No longer like old times. We were warriors in the days of our fathers.' His hitherto impassive face showed a flickering of sadness. 'I watch out of sight of *blancos*. Old Apache skill.'

'Can you describe any of the white men?'

The Apache drew his hands down his body to indicate clothing.

'*Vaqueros*,' he said;

'All dressed as cowboys?'

'*Si*. One man, fat – *mustachio grande colorado*,' the Apache said, placing a finger under his nose.

A fat man with a big red moustache: Pete Hazen without a doubt, thought Young. He had no reason to doubt that the Apache told the truth. Now he was learning rapidly. Now he knew most definitely that the deaths of the two unknown strangers and Dick, the discarding of their bodies and horse trappings and the concealing of the dead horses in the cave was the work of Guisewell's hirelings. Everything Karl Hessell had told him in Blue Mesa hours ago was confirmed.

Then the Apache sprang a surprise on him. He slipped his hand into the top of his breech cloth and withdrew a strip of grubby paper. He handed it to Young.

'From the two horses yonder,' he stated.

Intrigued, Young studied it. It was merely a crumpled

scrap, clearly torn from what must have been a letterhead and it bore an incomplete portion of a printed address:

CORPORATION, ASSAYERS OF MINERALS AND MINING
CONSULTANTS
DENVER
COLORADO TERRITORY

Young could not control a startled gasp.

'You found this near the two horses lying together?' he queried.

'*Si.* I guard this place because it is long time honoured by The People, but mostly I keep out of sight.'

Young felt that the veil between his own brash world and that of the ancient inhabitants of the land had been lifted a little. By 'The People', the Apache meant his own tribe. It was a term universally used by Indians, indicating the belief that their tribal group alone were the true human beings.

This lone guardian must be an elder who had escaped the scatterings and banishments to reservations and now watched over an old sacred place.

He had done Young a considerable service. Young now knew that the two men whose disappearance was being investigated by his brother were assayers. Doubtless they were in the Crouching Lion region to prospect for any presence of minerals, possibly silver, which was currently much sought after in the West and the discovery of which had created mushrooming, brawling boom towns in Arizona and New Mexico.

Young supposed the scrap of paper must have somehow fallen from a saddlebag as the trappings of the dead horses were removed. He made to hand it back but the Apache shook his head.

'You keep. Evidence for lawman.'

Young sought to clarify points concerning the exact details of the three killings.

'All three, how were they killed?' he asked

The Apache pointed to the boulders and rocks beneath the rock wall across the trail.

'First *ambuscadero* yonder, two *hombres blancos* killed. Rifles,' he stated.

'The first two were ambushed by rifle fire from the rocks across the trail,' translated Young.

'*Si*. Maybe one moon later, same white men arrive. *Ambuscadero* again. Rifles again. One *hombre blanco*, all alone, killed. Body in chasm.' Again the Indian jerked his thumb back to indicate the great fissure in the earth behind him.

Young damped down his angry emotions to form a clear picture of the bloody events at Crouching Lion from the Apache's vivid narrative. There had been two ambushes from the tumbled rocks lining one side of the trail. In each case, the perpetrators of the murders were W Bar G hands, with Pete Hazen prominent among them.

The two assayers were killed in the first attack and Dick Young was the victim of the second, about a month later. All three bodies were cast into the chasm and the horses, being too bulky to be quickly disposed of in that way, were shoved into the cave as a temporary measure, and he had been told by Cal Davis that Walt Guisewell wished to get rid of some 'evidence' at Crouching Lion.

This 'evidence' could only be the carcasses of the three horses that now lay mouldering in the cave.

'What happened after these shootings and, as I take it, after the horses were hauled into the cave?' Young asked.

The Apache pointed south. 'Men rode off. Too many white men and too many guns for one Apache so I keep well down in chasm but able to watch. Old skill of Apache again.'

Young gave an understanding nod. A bunch of whites of the calibre of Walt Guisewell's hands would have little compunction in quickly disposing of a lone Apache who had witnessed their activities. The ghosts of many a white victim could attest to the uncanny ability of the still free Apaches, skilled in hunting, to be almost invisible while lying in ambush beside a desert trail. Young raised his hand in an indication of peace again.

'I'm obliged to you,' he said gravely. 'I understand how the sacredness of this place has been violated. The white man's law will be put into action.'

The Apache's copper-hued face had resumed its composure. He pointed to the sky, then moved a finger in a circular motion as if indicating the atmosphere around them, then he pointed down to the ground.

'Spirits of sky, air and earth act soon. Work of all – the *hombres blancos* and The People – soon wiped out. Only power of the Great Spirit endures. See?' He pointed south to the sky above the far peaks of the Sierra Guadalupe.

Young screwed his eyes against the sun and saw a single, almost minuscule black cloud on the wide, faultless azure expanse of the sky.

'You prophesy a storm?' he asked.

'*Si*. Old skill again.'

Young wanted the answer to a further question.

'If any of the men who killed here were brought to

court, would you give evidence of what you saw?'

The Apache shook his head most emphatically.

'No. White men's courts never believe Apache. Apache not citizen – no rights.' He looked at Young and, as if emphasizing that a friendship had developed between them, he added confidentially, 'Anyway, this Apache defies *blanco* law and dodges reservation to guard old sacred place.'

Young said he understood. If there ever would be a day when the Native American people were granted US citizenship, it lay far in the future and, though the bulk of the tribes were now peaceful, 'The People' as a whole were not trusted.

As to the Apache being off the reservation to guard a place of ancient mystic repute, Young declared that he would not say a word. He raised his right hand, palm open, in the old gesture of peaceful intent.

The Apache returned the sign of peace, then walked away into the rocks along the top of the chasm and demonstrated that old Apache skill: of quickly becoming invisible.

Young rode away from Crouching Lion feeling that his quest was, in part, fulfilled. Many of the questions that had bedevilled him were answered. He knew the whereabouts of his brother's body; he vowed he would eventually retrieve it.

Furthermore, he knew something of the background of the two men whose disappearance Dick had been investigating, and he knew that Guisewell's hands were responsible for the villainy on the trail beside the chasm.

Those animal carcasses, both with their identifying brand and one with the scrap of paper as clues to the identities of the men from the assay office, could seal the fates of Walt Guisewell, who had masterminded the crimes at Crouching Lion, and his employees who had carried them out.

Two vital questions still had to be answered. Why had Guisewell organized the killing of the men from the assay office in the first place? And why had he followed it up with the murder of Dick Young, who had come to investigate their disappearance?

In some way that he could not define, Bob Young felt his meeting with the Apache guardian of the sacred site and the Indian's casting of his spell in the evocative atmosphere of Crouching Lion added up to a mystical experience emanating from some power beyond the invisible curtain of time separating his own era from that of those who earlier had walked the earth.

Young wondered if he was bewitched. But, if he was under some age-old enchantment that the minds of modern settlers in this raw land could not comprehend, what he had learned at Crouching Lion took his probing into the riddle of the three men who disappeared there a good deal further.

Now he was a man emerging from a trance, back in his own time and returning to Blue Mesa, where danger was imminent – if it had not already burst upon the town in an explosion of death and destruction.

CHAPTER TWELVE

BRING ON YOUR FIGHT!

Walt Guisewell believed he had his whole strategy worked out as he rode through the W Bar G ranch yard's wide gateway of peeled mesquite poles. He was at the head of a heavily armed column of horsemen. His full complement of hands was present and each was armed to the teeth.

It was true that Cal Davis was missing. He had skipped the ranch as the place slept but Guisewell considered Davis of no account anyway. Reasonably new to the outfit, he was somewhat dim-witted and had never properly fitted into the camaraderie of the bunkhouse. The W Bar G was well rid of him.

The men backing the rancher were tried and trusted hardcases. All had survived a variety of spectacular exploits of gunsmoke and bullets in earlier life. All were content to tug their forelocks to the imperious Guisewell and trigger their weapons on his behalf in return for his big wages.

Guisewell, now recovered from the deflating of his self-importance brought on by the visit from Young, commanded them like a general heading for battle. When the party reached the edge of Blue Mesa, it changed its formation so that he did not ride at its head. He sat his saddle in the middle of a long-strung-out line of riders, for his plan was to spring a gun-trap.

He would challenge Young from the middle of the line; then, while the gunfighter responded with his attention on the rancher, probably drawing his weapon if he had not already done so, the men on either end of the line would act in unison and gun Young down.

Looking forward to playing his part in this treachery was Fats Anderson, the cowhand with the paunch and straggling moustache, who had shown signs of contemplating gunplay against Young in the Lucky Dollar but had backed down. He was on the far right of the line. He was eager but cautious. He resolved to have his Colt already drawn but concealed before the riders met up with Young.

On the extreme left of the other wing of the horsemen, charged with firing on Young at the same time as Anderson, was gangling Slim Forster. He was a different proposition from Anderson, more cunning but essentially scared of Young, whom he had known as Hank Teed.

Guisewell's fire-eating talk had geared the riders to believe that everything would go their way in this venture.

Walt Guisewell rode pretty much as he did when out on the range with his rannies, with only light saddle trappings: his coiled lariat and a carbine in a scabbard, but he carried a pair of curious extra burdens. On either side of his saddle there was a leather pannier, each obviously heavily laden.

The W Bar G party rode on, stirring the dust in the direction of Blue Mesa. It was past noon now. The heat of the mercilessly beating sun was stifling, and the ever present flies buzzed around the heads of the horses.

No one noticed the slowly growing black cloud high over the peaks of the Guadalupe range far to the south.

Since taking a brief rest at Split Rock Sink the riders had been undergoing mingled sensations of rising bloodlust and cautious apprehension about the task ahead of them. Now, after cresting a rise, they could see the buildings of Blue Mesa coming into view. In a short time they would be trooping into the town's single street.

At precisely the same time, at the far end of the street, Bob Young was riding in, warily and with sharp-eyed vigilance.

All was totally still. Blue Mesa seemed to be what it always was: an ugly frontier township with its main street today devoid of people and animals to a degree even more eerie than usual.

Obviously, nothing untoward had happened yet. Nevertheless, Young would not be lulled into thinking that Walt Guisewell's fiery talk was mere bluster.

He paced his mount along the street and reached the Mesa House. Suddenly the figure of Rube Cousins emerged from the alley beside the hotel. He was carrying a Winchester and had a warlike-looking bandolier of carbine shells slanted across his chest.

Young pulled rein as Cousins walked towards him.

'All seems quiet, Rube,' he commented.

'Don't be fooled. There's a blow-up on the way for sure, and folks are beginning to form up against all-out trouble; they're all four-square against Guisewell,' Cousins replied. 'There's someone with a shooting-iron behind every window in town and some fellows are even sprawled on the roofs, out of sight and with rifles and shotguns. I'm posting myself right here in the alley to protect my place if anyone tries to shoot it up.

'Even little old Doc McTavish showed up with his black bag and asked me to let him have one of my back rooms where he can set up a clinic,' he went on. 'He said he knew this town had written him off as a hopeless old drunk but, if folks get hurt, he'd show 'em he was still a damned sight smarter than the latest graduate from any medical college back East.

'Rosita has volunteered to help him. Like most Mexican women she don't scare easily.' Cousins gave a throaty chuckle, then added:

'And guess what I heard a few minutes ago. Our gallant Marshal Ezra Todd and his deputy Horace Slack blew town by a back trail early this morning. They're Guisewell's men and know the townsfolk have no time for them. So, if the W Bar B bunch show up, out to disturb the peace, you can bet your boots Todd and Slack wouldn't have the guts to even pretend to arrest them.'

'Running out is just about what I'd expect of them,' Young replied. 'They knew plenty about the dirty work at Crouching Lion but were too damned scared of Guisewell to spill the beans.'

'Sure,' grunted Cousins. 'They were only Guisewell's tame puppy dogs. As for peacekeeping, any show of strength came from the W Bar G roughnecks, and it was unlawful strength at that. And that ain't all. The three who came in from Sandy Crossing are staying and itching for a fight.' He chuckled as if itching for a fight himself. 'They'd like to see Guisewell given his come-uppance. They're making themselves scarce in the alleyway alongside the

Ace Café. In fact, darned near the whole town is keeping out of sight and laying for Guisewell's bunch.'

He gave an ironic laugh. 'Funny thing is that the towns-folk don't find it easy to live in his town, but their dander is up because he threatened to shoot up the place. I guess, after all, that's because their homes are here.'

Young suddenly stared along the street and his hand automatically took up its habitual position above his pistol butt. Some stirrings at the far end of the street caught his attention.

A cloud of hoof-raised dust was showing distantly as the drumming sound of approaching horses grew louder.

Rube Cousins ran back to the shelter of the alley to take up his position. Young came after him on horseback, swerved the animal into the area behind the hotel where the stable stood. He leapt from the saddle and hastily led the horse into its accustomed stall, leaving it facing the feed box, still saddled and with all its accoutrements in place.

He snatched his carbine from its saddle scabbard and ran back down the alley. At the end of it Cousins was holding his defensive position, facing the street.

'Don't shoot too early, Rube,' Young panted as he passed the hotel proprietor. 'Wait until they give you cause. And don't shoot Guisewell. I want him hauled into court – alive!'

He planted himself at the edge of the boardwalk, close to the alley's entrance and watched the street with nar-rowed eyes. Slowly, there came into view the long line of horsemen, riding abreast and strung across the full width of the street. The sun put a glint on weapons already drawn and ready for deadly business.

Behind the riders the wide sky was slowly darkening and more grey clouds were bunching as if setting the backdrop for an unfolding drama to be acted out on the street below.

Young viewed the street immediately before him in the manner of a military commander considering the field on which he was about to do battle; he eyed the strong features in his favour and noted the hazards that might act against his interests.

He saw that, along the boardwalk, some distance from him, arranged outside a store beyond the Mesa House, was a row of large and substantial wooden packing cases and barrels.

A man might find a comfortable bolt-hole behind the cases and barrels if a gunfight went against him, he conjectured, and he would be well placed to fire on anyone in the middle of the street.

He quickly assessed the positions of the riders as they grew larger in his vision: Guisewell was in the centre of the line with his faithful foreman, Pete Hazen, beside him. Both rode with the arrogance of triumphant conquerors, a pomposity that Young itched to deflate while, at the same time, wanting both of them to live and, one day, face a court of constitutional justice.

The witness from Sandy Crossing had definitely identified Hazen as having been among the riders he saw heading for Crouching Lion prior to the disappearances, and the Apache had identified a man with a big red moustache. This made Young sure of Hazen's involvement in the villainy at Crouching Lion.

He had no concrete proof to show that Walt Guisewell had been a member of the bushwhacking parties on either fateful day, but he was in no doubt that the rancher's scheming mind had devised the murders perpetrated on both occasions.

Young walked towards the oncoming rancher and his band. He halted close to where the packing cases and the barrels were placed. He ceased walking and watched the approach of the horsemen, keeping himself stock still and with his right hand in its ready position above his holstered gun butt. His Winchester carbine was cradled under his left arm. He appeared to the invading riders to be the only human figure standing on the silent street.

The W Bar G men were totally unaware that the sweaty torpidity of the day matched an unseen, heated and brooding resentment of Walt Guisewell among a considerable number of Blue Mesa's citizens, for which reason a number of them were at that moment armed and waiting behind shuttered windows or concealed in alleys and on roofs.

If Guisewell's rage was so ungovernable that he would cause destruction in the town he had founded, the little people dwelling there, whom the rancher considered of no account, would not permit the destruction of their homes and all they owned. The anger engendered by the rancher's overbearing attitude, which they had endured for too long, was a catalyst, working drastic changes in the people of Blue Mesa and destroying any respect they once had for him.

Young stood still beside the boardwalk, watching Guisewell and his line of riders coming forward at the trot. He noted that the rancher had his carbine in his hands and was all ready for action. He eyed with interest the pair of leather panniers riding on either side of his saddle.

Walt Guisewell uttered a growling command and the riders halted in a long string, spanning the street from side to side. Guisewell sat in very centre of the line He hooted a challenge at Young:

'Young, you've made a damned nuisance of yourself in this country – *my* country – strutting around and making out you have some kind of grievance with me. Well, let's settle the matter for good and all *now*. Bring it on!'

All along Young had realized that the positioning of the W Bar G Riders in relation to where he stood had all the makings of a gun-trap. He was aware that the men at either end of the line were primed to kill him where he stood and, if he moved to face Guisewell, in the middle of the mounted line, the extreme ends of the two wings would quickly move around to trap him as in a pincer movement and he would be at the mercy of the guns of the entire crew.

He quickly looked along the strung-out line, saw a gallery of hard-bitten faces, tensed and ready for action and he knew that one of the riders would make a premature move, signalling the intention of the whole bunch.

It came from the last rider on the extreme left of the line, the squat man with the paunch who had been thwarted in his move to draw on Young in the Lucky Dollar.

Fats Anderson, who had been briefed to open the trap on Young simultaneously with Forster at the opposite end of the line, was prodded by an irksome restlessness he could control no longer. It caused him to dance his mount forward prematurely and lift a fist already grasping his naked Colt six-gun.

His face twisted by a fury that had raged inside him ever since Young made him back down in the saloon, he levelled the pistol at Young with what he imagined was a swift action.

Young made a dizzyingly speedy move for his holster and his hand swept upwards, bearing a bucking, barking Colt, spitting unerring fire at Anderson.

Anderson lurched back in the saddle with an almost surprised gurgle. He flung his revolver into the air, then he jerked forward to sprawl lifeless over his saddle horn.

The incident caused a momentary collective paralysis among the Guisewell riders. Young launched himself on speeding legs along the boardwalk, with his carbine in one hand and his Colt in the other. He sought his pre-selected bolt-hole: the shelter of the barrels and packing cases outside the store.

He lay on his back on the scuffed planks, shoved his Colt back into its holster and pumped his Winchester.

Looking up, he saw the sky growing even darker with more leaden clouds banking over the roofs of Blue Mesa although the air remained torrid and without a breath of wind.

Sheltered by the packing cases and barrels he was out of the sight of Guisewell's mounted raiders, who were now embroiled in a turbulent mêlée in the middle of the street only yards from him. There was a blasting of gunfire and the sounds of shuffling, snorting horses and human yelps of pain. For the moment at least, Guisewell seemed to be too preoccupied to think about his duel with Young.

With his Winchester at the ready, Young looked over the top of a barrel and saw that the earlier cocksure arrogance of the W Bar G attackers had been crushed completely under steadily sustained firing from the other side of the street.

Guisewell and his horsemen were being tossed around in a panicky swirl of horseflesh amidst an acrid fog of gun fumes. They seemed to be in such a state of blind confusion that they were unable to fire any adequate answering lead towards those who were attacking them.

Young realized that the shooting was coming from the workshop of Tom Gross, the blacksmith. Judging by the rate of fire, there was evidently a second marksman concealed inside the smithy with Gross.

The scramble of beleaguered riders was hardly yards away from the edge of the boardwalk where Young lay under cover and another opponent of the Guisewell faction on a high rooftop let fly with a carbine shell which screamed into the roiling mayhem. A man who was on the left of Guisewell's line of riders, which had now fallen into total disarraty, gave a howl of pain and clutched at his cheek, which was spurting blood.

He happened to be Slim Forster, who would have acted simultaneously with Fats Anderson in springing a gun-trap on Young but for Anderson's going off at half-cock. He fell to one side in the saddle as his steed was buffeted by other bucking, plunging horses.

Then he was thrown. He dropped the pistol he was flourishing as he was sent sprawling against the boardwalk, so close to the cases and barrels giving cover to Young that he almost knocked them over.

Young laid down his carbine, drew his Colt and shoved a packing case to one side. Doubled almost in two he moved forward, clutched Forster's shirt collar with his free hand and hauled him back to the walk.

Forster, with both hands pressed to his heavily bleeding face, seemed not to know what was happening. Young took a speedy glance at the action in the middle of the street. There he could see a confusion of cursing, grunting men and hear the snorting and whinnying of animals. The heaving mass of riders and mounts was cloaked by a swirling cloud of dust.

He saw that most of the riders were urging their mounts to ride away along the street to escape this spot where they had encountered such unrelenting opposition. Guisewell, obviously unhurt, was sprawled low along his animal's back, spurring it to put himself in the lead.

Young planted Forster on his back on the boards behind the barrier of barrels and cases. Forster took a hand away from his blood-soaked face, looked at Young and shuddered. He was in the clutches of the man he remembered as Hank Teed, the dynamic, quick-triggered deputy lawman of Twin Boulders

He had seen Teed in action in Wyoming; now he had just witnessed his lightning speed in dispatching Fats Anderson, who had faced him with his gun already drawn. The man with the tied-down holster scared Forster down to the very last inch of his guts.

As Young and Forster lay alongside each other in this reasonably secure refuge from the turmoil in the middle of the street the wounded man felt the mouth of a Colt revolver pressed against his temple. His blood ran cold with the fear that Young was about to shoot him then and there.

'I'm hit,' he croaked piteously. 'Dammit, I'm hit!'

'You won't die from it,' growled Young, increasing the pressure of his weapon against the side of Forster's head. 'I want information and I want it fast. What is Guisewell planning, aside from his crackpot notion of getting me even if it means shooting up the town? He's carrying a pair of panniers. What's in them?'

'Explosives,' gabbled. Forster. 'Them new-fangled sticks from Europe that miners put into rocks to blow them up.'

CHAPTER THIRTEEN

DYNAMITE

'*Dynamite!*' gasped Young. 'Do you mean dynamite?'

'Yes, dynamite. He aims to push on to Crouching Lion to destroy something there. He wants to get rid of it by blowing it up.'

Young set his mouth in a tight line. Dynamite, developed some years previously in Europe by the chemist Nobel, was fairly new on the scene of the American West; it was used mainly by engineers and railroad-construction teams.

Now, with his brain working overtime, Young thought back to what he knew of the murderous events at Crouching Lion. He recalled Slim Davis, the deserter from the W Bar G, telling him about the rumour current around the ranch: that there was some 'evidence' at Crouching Lion Guisewell wished to be rid of.

'What's this thing at Crouching Lion that's bugging Guisewell?' he demanded. 'I know some of your outfit were at Crouching Lion some time back. Were you with them? What were they up to?'

'I don't know. I wasn't with them. There was only a few, chosen by Guisewell – Pete Hazen, Fats Anderson and some others. Guisewell didn't go with them. They went a couple of times and stayed away three or four nights at a time.'

Young recalled Karl Hessell saying he'd seen Forster in the party heading in the direction of Crouching Lion. He felt in his guts that Forster was lying when he denied having any part in the killings there. The W Bar G rider doubtless envisaged hangings if Young found solid proof of the bushwhackings at the deep chasm and he was scared almost out of his wits.

Young, preoccupied with the ruckus on the street, saw that this was not the time or place to push the issue, but he vowed he'd get the truth out of Forster sooner or later.

As it was, he was finding that the happenings at Crouching Lion were beginning to take coherent shape in his mind. The 'evidence' that so concerned Guisewell could only be the remains of the horses dumped in the cave. The remnants bearing the brand of the Sandy Crossing livery stable and the scrap of printed letterhead bore eloquent witness to the fate of the men from the assay company.

Forster, sprawled on the boardwalk, his face running with blood, was without a weapon and he was consumed by fear, knowing he was at the mercy of Young who had stacked up a reputation as a swift hand with a gun.

Young realized that the sounds of mounted activity and shooting on the street had abruptly ceased, except for a couple of shots from the direction of the blacksmith's forge. He rose and, crouching, looked over the barrier of the barrels and cases, and found that the horde of battling riders had moved away. Three W Bar G men lay dead in the dust while another couple were afoot and staggering around, obviously wounded.

He was just in time to witness the tail end of the W Bar G troop disappearing into an alley on the far side of the street; he realized what their strategy was. They were seeking safety at the back of the built-up street. Blue Mesa was a one-street town. There was nothing behind the rows of buildings lining either side of the street but wide-open semi-desert.

Obviously, the response of the armed citizenry to Guisewell's attack had proved too much for the mounted party. The many determined defenders posted at unexpected points, and the knowledge that there must be more in wait if they tried to make headway along the street, had driven the W Bar G men to seek refuge from the dangers of the thoroughfare. Hence they had bolted down an alley-way to reach the back of the buildings.

Young wondered whether the W Bar G men would ride back to the ranch or head the other way, towards Crouching Lion, so that Guisewell could fulfil his mission with his load of dynamite. Surely the decision to use the explosive must be the rancher's choice, since the need to destroy the incriminating evidence was obviously a nagging anxiety to him.

He looked up, wondering why the sun was beginning to lose its ferocity and, for the first time, grasped the meaning of the rapid changes that had been taking place in the sky over the Texas line. Where there had been flawless azure there was a leaden greyness and banks of black cloud were rolling towards Blue Mesa. Rain was coming – and coming soon.

He reasoned that Guisewell and his crew would surely make for Crouching Lion: they were probably already riding full pelt at the rear of the buildings on the opposite side of the street. If he slipped down an alley to the rear of his own side of the street and ran along the back of the properties, he would reach the rear of the Mesa House where his horse was stabled.

The woebegone Slim Forster lay to one side of him, with his hands against his face. Young bent, grabbed him by the shirt and hauled him to his feet. The man was utterly defeated, wounded, terrified and seemed to be bewildered.

'Get yourself down to the Mesa House,' ordered Young. 'Doc McTavish is there. He'll fix that wound. And, by God, I'll catch up with you and find out what you know about the Crouching Lion antics. Don't you forget it.'

Then, holding his Winchester, he ran down the board-walk and into the nearest alley, scooting through it to the open land. The relatively short run along the back of the clapboard and adobe buildings brought him to the yard of the Mesa House. He bolted into it, then into the stables where his horse stood with its only stablemate, Rube Cousins's mount.

While Young was collecting his already saddled horse Rube Cousins appeared from the neighbouring alley, looking sorely disappointed.

'What's happening?' he asked. 'There was a powerful amount of shooting at the other end of the street but nothing has happened here. Where's Guisewell? I want to have a crack at him.'

'If he and his bunch haven't already shown up from the behind the other side of the street and gone chasing off to Crouching Lion, they're about to appear,' shouted Young. He ran out of the stable, leading his horse. 'Though maybe he's thrown his hand in and gone in the other direction, back to the W Bar G. But I doubt it.'

'On the other side of the street?' echoed Cousins. 'Hell, the three from Sandy Crossing and Cooty Sawkins are over there, in the alley beside the Ace Café. If Guisewell's bunch had showed up there we'd have heard about it.'

He and Young were not to know that, at the rear of the buildings across the street, the Guisewell riders had halted their flight for a brief spell so that their horses could catch up on their breathing after the turmoil on the street. Conscious that even in this deserted area behind the buildings they might be targets for snipers on the rooftops, Guisewell had insisted on the mounted group pulling into a tight knot against the back of a store.

They huddled close to the clapboard walls, a dejected bunch of men on panting and steaming horses, everyone acutely aware of the imminent possibility of shots being loosed upon them by well-concealed rooftop marksmen.

Out of the midst of the dispirited horsemen came an objection to the plan Guisewell hoped to put into action. It was uttered by none other than Pete Hazen, the rancher's usually slavishly loyal foreman. Hazen was weary, also he was recovering from the shock of a near miss by a bullet, which had torn a rent in a shirtsleeve but had not harmed him.

In his view, Guisewell's venture into Blue Mesa had been a failure from the very start. Bob Young had turned the tables on the W Bar G party instead of falling into the gun-trap set for him. Then there had followed the treachery of the citizens, who demonstrated with hot lead that they would no longer permit themselves to be crushed under the rancher's heels.

Pete Hazen was shaken by the way things had turned

out and his loyalty was wavering. So he used the weather as an excuse to propose abandoning Guisewell's declared next move: a ride to Crouching Lion so that the rancher could attend to what he insisted was pressing business.

Hazen pointed to the louring leaden sky, now casting a gloom over Blue Mesa.

'Mr Guisewell, the weather's about to break,' he ventured cautiously. 'In a minute we'll have rain, one of them desert downpours usual after a hot spell. Maybe we should call the whole thing quits.'

There was a general grunt of approval from the group.

There was some value in Hazen's objection. After weeks of blazing sunshine and conditions of near drought, the breaking of the weather in this corner of the desert flatlands invariably meant a sudden storm of torrential rain, slashing down on the land with bullet-like force. From his years of experience Guisewell well knew the punishment desert weather conditions could inflict, but he was obsessed with other considerations and in no mood to listen to any suggestion that he be deflected from his purpose.

He was the only one who was not sitting deflated in his saddle. He was posed there with stubborn dignity, his face dark with anger matching the threatening skies, and with his brows lowered over glittering eyes. He was gripped by a blazing obsession.

'Quits be damned!' he roared. 'You mean *you* want to quit! Well, none of you will quit. Why do you think I pay you far more than you'll ever make on any cow outfit in creation? You'll ride with me to Crouching Lion until I have attended to things there.' He slapped one of the leather panniers in front of his saddle and added, in a cracked, slightly hysterical note, 'Then, we'll come back here and settle the hash of this damned town. C'mon, let's ride!'

He turned his horse's head around to face the far end of the street, where the rear of the Ace Café and the alley running alongside it were located. This was the extreme limit of Blue Mesa's single street: beyond that point there was only open desert and the trail leading the Crouching Lion.

Spurring his mount, Guisewell led the horsemen at as fast a clip as could be managed by animals that had already been through some gruelling physical action. The riders took care to continue hugging the backs of the buildings for fear of snipers.

It happened that Young, leading his horse and accompanied by Rube Cousins, had just crossed the street and speeded into the alley. Here they had met up with Cooty Sawkins, who was with Willows, Cornford and Hessell, the trio from Sandy Crossing. All four were armed and feeling somewhat cheated at missing the action in the other end of the street.

They heard the thump of the W Bar G Horses coming nearer, approaching the other end of the alleyway where it gave on to the open land at the back of the stores. They all rushed to that point, arriving at just the very moment that Guisewell and his men reached it. The horsemen were spurring the best speed they could out of steeds that had already endured gruelling experiences.

The half-dozen men in the alley let loose a surprise blast of firing to welcome the riders as they pounded past the alley. There was a yell of pain as one of their number stopped a bullet but the W Bar G party continued on the hoof without answering the shots. They were quickly clear of Blue Mesa and following Walt Guisewell in the direction of Crouching Lion. Little Cooty Sawkins, flourishing his Winchester, spat in disgust.

'Doggone it!' he bellowed. 'They went past like a tornado. I only got one shot in. Dammit! I'm getting my cayuse and going after them. I'm not passing up a chance to fix Guisewell and his bunch for good.'

'I'm with you,' enthused Rube Cousins, who was as belligerent – and as old – as the café proprietor 'My horse is stabled back at the hotel. I'll run back there and saddle him.'

Young, already mounted and raring to pursue the W Bar G men, cautioned the two older men:

'Cooty, Rube, with all due respect to your grey hairs, you'd be better off here. I aim to go after Guisewell and his crew because I have a pretty big axe to grind,' he stated. 'It'll be hard-going over a heap of rough country and Guisewell is planning some dirty work with some dynamite at Crouching Lion. Anyway, take a look at the sky. The weather is ready to break at any minute.'

'Blast it! You're telling us we're too old to carry on the fight?' objected Rube Cousins loudly.

'And that's far from the truth,' said Cooty Sawkins. 'I've got my dander up good and strong. I feel as fit to fight as I did at twenty.'

'Instead of arguing, why not set about putting things to rights here in town?' suggested Young soberly from his saddle. 'The worthless officers of the law have vamoosed. Guisewell's people are lying in the street: some are dead and others wounded. Doc McTavish is patching people up and probably needs help, and the W Bar G men in our hands need guarding. We have to put them into a properly constituted court at some time. Put the wounded in the marshal's cells and have Doc McTavish work on them. Then deliver the dead to the undertaker.'

Cousins and Sawkins, mollified, indicated that they saw merit in Young's suggestions. Young added a last stipulation:

'Keep your eyes on that Forster joker. I'll want some answers from him later.' He spurred his horse and headed for the end of the alley but Sam Willows, from Sandy Crossing, grabbed the animal's bridle to restrain it.

'Hold hard! Harry, Karl and I are coming with you.' he said. 'We have our quarrels with Guisewell, too. And, anyway, Crouching Lion is on our way home. Our horses are hitched just the other side of the café.'

'Well, make haste,' urged Young. 'Let's quit wasting time. Guisewell will be heading for Crouching Lion. He's carrying dynamite and he's aiming to use it there. It's all too complicated to explain now.'

Five minutes later, backed by the mounted Willows, Cornford and Hessell, he pounded out of the alley. The four spurred their animals to follow the path of the W Bar G men at speed.

Just as they departed from Blue Mesa the first growling rumble of thunder was heard from the distant Guadalupe range.

Then the rumbling became menacing claps of thunder, loud as firecrackers, sounding almost overhead.

CHAPTER FOURTEEN

NIGHT PURSUIT

Young and his three companions had a couple of advantages over the party they pursued. Their horses were fresh whereas those of Guisewell and his men had endured the wearying turmoil of the action on the street of Blue Mesa and their subsequent hasty departure from the town.

Secondly, the three men from Sandy Crossing had a close familiarity with the tract of country between Blue Mesa and Crouching Lion. They knew some short cuts by way of obscure trails of which Young would be unaware.

'Remember, boys,' Young shouted from his saddle, 'if we get close to this bunch, they'll want to shoot it out, but it'd be best to grab them alive. I want to see all those responsible for the killings answer to a court; Guisewell in particular because I know he was behind the whole scheme.'

'A tall order,' commented Karl Hessell. 'If that bunch starts shooting there'll be nothing half-hearted about it.'

'I know, but they'll be weary by now after the ruckus

in the town, and they lost some men,' Young pointed out. 'We don't know how many are left. After the licking they took they might just be ready to listen to some reasoning. Though it's a slight chance – Guisewell's behaving like he's crazy. There's evidence in the cave near Crouching Lion and he's determined to blow it up.'

Sam Willows, jogging beside Young observed, 'With some of them facing the gallows, I reckon they won't be in a mood to powwow when they can shoot.'

'I reckon so too, but I'm always optimistic,' declared Young.

Young led his three companions onwards over the open desert under a darkening sky lit by the occasional fork of white lightning while the claps of thunder grew ever louder. Then the heavens suddenly opened and huge drops of rain began to fall.

In next to no time the downpour had increased its intensity, lashing men and beasts with such force that it seemed intent on penetrating their skins. All four horsemen yanked their hats down almost to their eyes and rode with their upper bodies bent so far forward and heads so low that their chins nearly touched their saddle horns.

They tried to discern the dim trail through the curtains of rain as their horses shuddered and snorted nervously and thunder blasted the sky with the power of artillery fire. Well after leaving Blue Mesa the party still could see no trace of Guisewell's riders.

Harry Cornford shouted over the sound of the downpour. 'Maybe they've sheltered from the rain. There's a side trail just ahead and it leads to a bunch of big rocks, some big enough to give some shelter to men and cayuses. Maybe we should head that way?'

'Could be worth trying, providing we'd still be heading directly for Crouching Lion,' agreed Young.

'We will,' Cornford assured him. 'In fact, it's a short cut. If we don't meet up with them on that trail it could take us to Crouching Lion before they arrive if they go by the longest way.'

It was not yet fully dusk but the stormy sky put the whole landscape under a curtain of gloom and the hunched men kept to a plodding pace while the rain pelted them with wet bullets. All four kept their eyes skinned for the opening of the side trail until Harry Cornford gave a hoarse yell of triumph on spotting a familiar landmark.

'Here it is, boys – off to our right.'

They swung their horses' heads around and took a narrow and hardly discernible narrow trail. It snaked between clumps of Spanish dagger and stands of cactus. The sodden ground made uncertain footing for the animals' hoofs and was scattered with rocks of assorted sizes.

Then, with the typically unpredictable moodiness of desert weather, the rain abruptly stopped and the last of the thunder clattered away across the land. Young and his companions, although soaked to the skin, heaved sighs of relief. After the long spell of ovenlike heat, the downpour had lightened the air and there was a whisper of cooling breeze.

'I know this trail; those rocks you talked about are not far from where it begins,' said Karl Hessell to Cornford.

'That's right. Not too far from where we are now,' confirmed Cornford.

'Then take care,' cautioned Young. 'If they're holed-up there and they hear us coming, they might cut loose on us. They could have good cover in the rocks if it comes to a shoot-out.' His three companions took his point, unshipped their carbines from their saddle scabbards and rode on, their eyes trying to pierce the gloom to discover what lay only yards ahead of them.

After a spell of cautious plodding forward they rounded a twist in the trail.

'Rocks on the trail ahead,' Young called out.

He was standing in his stirrups and looking over the head of his horse at the prospect in front of the mounted party. Just discernible were a number of rocks of varying sizes, some almost small boulders, arranged in ragged alignment across the width of the trail to form a barrier. It was not a natural scattering of rocks. They had obviously been placed there by the labour of men.

A deposit of horse-droppings, obviously very recent, proved that there had been mounted men in the vicinity.

Young halted his mount, raising his hand to signal to his companions to do the same. He screwed his eyes to penetrate the dimness of falling dusk, and made out a rising cluster of boulders and cactus beyond the obstruction on the trail.

He saw at once that Guisewell and his party had certainly taken this obscure trail and must be aware of the possibility of being followed by a party from Blue Mesa. They had hauled the rocks on to the trail to obstruct the pursuit and it must have been done only a short time before, probably during the spell of heavy rain. Young drew his Colt with his usual lightning speed.

'Watch that pile pf rocks yonder,' he called. 'They could be holed-up there, waiting to pick us off while we're stopped by this barrier.'

'They've had enough time to do it,' said Sam Willows dubiously, 'and they haven't fired a shot yet.'

'Still, take care. They could be biding their time, sitting up there in the rocks and squinting down their sights at us,' warned Young as he climbed down from his saddle.

There was nothing they could do but clear the barrier of rocks from the trail if they were to continue their pursuit, even though there was imminent danger of sniper fire from the larger tumble of rocks while they were doing it. But, as yet, all was silence from that source.

Young quickly formed a plan of action and lost no time in implementing it. He, Sam Willows and Karl Hessell set about shifting the rock barrier to make enough of a gap for their horses to pass through, while Harry Cornford stationed himself on the trail with a ready carbine and kept watch on the danger point of the far rocks.

Moving the rocks speedily was not easy. Some larger ones required the strength of two of the men to budge them out of position, but the whole procedure was finished without the interruption of hostile bullets.

'Looks like they've gone ahead of us,' commented Young, panting as they finished the chore. 'They can't have had much of a rest here. Some of them must have spent the whole time lugging rocks around just to delay us.'

'And they couldn't have rested their tired horses much, either,' observed Karl Hessell, 'but they left us proof that they went this way, so we are right on their heels.'

'Well, there's nothing else to do but keep going right on, wet and plumb weary as we are,' Young said. He led his horse through the gap created in the barricade of rocks.

Darkness of night was gathering and he began to wonder, as he had when soldiering years before during pursuits of an intelligent and determined enemy over unfamiliar land: what hazards lay ahead? What possible strong points of terrain, offering cover for ambush? What opportunities for springing the element of surprise on the pursuers, and what was the strength and stamina of the pursued?

The ruse of blocking the trail could have afforded them only a slight advantage. On horses already weary, they might be much nearer than Young and his companions imagined.

'How far are we from where this trail joins the one to Crouching Lion, Sam?' Young asked Willows.

'Maybe five miles,' Willows said as he remounted. 'Right where the two trails join there's a water hole, and after the rain it'll be full. Any group of riders who've travelled as hard as Guisewell's gang has would surely stop there for the horses to drink. There's plenty of cover there – cactus and rocks. It could be another danger spot. I figure they'll just naturally choose it to ambush us.'

'I reckon you're right,' Young agreed. 'They just rigged up this rock barrier to delay us, but there's no water here and their cayuses need to drink. The water hole at the junction of the trails ahead sounds like a likely spot to hunker down and make a fight of it.'

'Could be a tough proposition,' put in Harry Cornford. 'We'll be meeting them in darkness and our own horses need water.'

'All the more reason to lick them if they make a stand at the water hole,' stated Young grimly. 'Let's ride, but keep your carbines ready. They'll have the advantage of the night to surprise us if they've reached the water hole before us and are lying in wait up there and hear us coming. So, we must use the night, too. If they suddenly open fire on us, dismount fast, crouch low on the trail to fire back but move your position after every shot. That'll confuse them.'

All four took their Winchesters from their saddle scabbards and rode onward as darkness enfolded the landscape with the abruptness usual on the desert. They progressed with caution, always alert to the possibility of encountering Guisewell's party on the open trail.

They plunged into the velvety blackness in which there was no possibility of finding a landmark. Minutes ticked away with no semblance of activity coming from the W Bar G men somewhere ahead.

'The junction must be quite close,' said Sam Willows in a low voice. No sooner had he spoken than a lance of white rifle-flame slashed through the darkness from an unseen point and a shell screamed through the group of pursuers without finding a victim.

'We're there! Down!' hissed Young.

There was a quick flurry of action as all four men vacated their saddles and crouched low on the trail. They answered with a ragged volley of carbine shots aimed at the apparent source of the attacking shot and were rewarded by the sound of ricochets echoing through rocks and cactus guarding the water hole, the exact location of which could only be guessed at.

Each man dutifully shifted his position after every shot, pumped his Winchester and fired again.

They heard their opponents spitting profanities and there was a startled whinnying of horses from the direction of the ambushers. It sounded as if something was happening at the water hole where the W Bar G men had established themselves.

Down on the dark trail, Young called softly, 'Everybody here? Nobody hurt?'

Reassuringly, positive answers came from three positions near to him in the black night. The firing from the water hole ceased and the men crouching on the trail maintained their positions, held their breaths and kept their rifles at the ready.

Then came a harsh growling of conversation, too distant to be understood; the clip-clop of horses on rocks and a jangle of ringbits. The sounds were rapidly diminishing.

'They're pulling out,' whispered Young.

'By thunder, they've had all the fight they want,' answered Karl Hessel triumphantly. Young had a more practical view.

'I reckon they're vamoosing because they're running short of ammunition. They used up a heap at Blue Mesa and they don't have an unlimited supply. I would remind you that neither have we. Use it sparingly from now on.'

'Do you figure they're still heading for Crouching Lion?' asked Harry Cornford.

'You can bet they are,' said Young. 'They can't turn back from here without another brawl with us and, anyway, Guisewell is plumb crazy set on doing his dirty work with that dynamite. We'll have to gather our horses and stay right behind them. I reckon Guisewell is nothing but a madman and not fit to be running around with a load of dynamite.'

CHAPTER FIFTEEN

DISSENSION ON THE HOOF

Obsessive and furious anger surged within Walt Guisewell. He urged his horse through the darkness of the trail to Crouching Lion as he and his men departed from the ambush point at the water hole.

Returning to the trail to Crouching Lion, mounted and beginning to jog away, he counted the heads of his party as best he could in the darkness. It was the first time since running from Blue Mesa in defeat that he had taken stock of his followers.

He was aware that he had started out from the ranch with eighteen men: the whole of his bunkhouse crew minus the deserter Davis. He knew he had lost some at Blue Mesa, either by death or wounding, but he had not taken a count of the full number of the casualties.

Now, in so far as he could count heads in the uncertain light, he discovered that two more riders had gone missing since the retreat from the town, so his followers now numbered nine.

'Where are Hartman and Potter?' he demanded harshly.

A pair of somewhat dubious strangers, riding together, Hartman and Potter had recently been added to the hefty payroll of W Bar G gunslicks. Guisewell took them to be the kind of pistol-packing hardcases he favoured, and he hired them without asking too many questions.

His query was met by silence.

'Where the hell are they?' Guisewell repeated on an almost hysterical note.

The voice of Pete Hazen answered querulously, revealing something he had feared to mention to the rancher.

'They sneaked away sometime after we blocked the trail with those rocks, Mr Guisewell. Potter claimed he was hit in the leg when we ran from Blue Mesa and he and Hartman belly-ached about being made to haul rocks when they were soaked by the rain. They kind of left the trail and must have gone off over the rough country.'

Walt Guisewell spat angrily. He dimly recalled hearing someone yelp with pain as the riders were fired on from the alleyway alongside the Ace Café at the edge of town, but he had been too absorbed by his obsessive fury to pay attention to the welfare of his men.

'Blasted no-account saddle tramps!' he spluttered. 'First that worthless Davis ups and quits, now Hartman and Potter – who were not worth a damn in the first place – skulk away. I figure most of you are yellow when the cards are down.'

Then he turned his fury on his foreman who had hitherto considered himself to be so loyal.

'Damn you, Hazen! It was you who infected this crew with yellow fever in the first place.'

'Me?' croaked Hazen, all injured innocence. 'What did I do?'

'I haven't forgotten it was you who squawked about quitting right after we took a setback at Blue Mesa – and it *was* only a setback because I aim to go back and make that blasted town suffer. You put the idea of running for it into the brainless heads of those damned saddle tramps.'

'But *I* didn't quit, Mr Guisewell,' bleated Hazen in a toadying whine. 'I stuck with you and I'm still sticking with you.'

'And don't think I don't know why,' snarled the rancher. 'When that damned, gutless fool Horace Slack came to the W Bar G yelling about Young showing up at Todd's office, saying he was out to get the truth of what happened at Crouching Lion and settling it at law – state law, not Blue Mesa law – you got plumb scared. You could see yourself facing the gallows at the end of the trail. You stick with the bunch because you want the protection of their guns around you.'

He turned in the saddle, glowered at the riders and snarled, 'I suppose the whole damned crew of you are sticking together because you're scared of the rope, or else you'd all have quitting fever. There's only a handful on our tail and we can't spend any more lead on hoping to hold them back by firing into darkness. We'll fight them off when we can see them. C'mon, speed up those horses. We have work to do.'

The nine spurred their already tired horses, every man inwardly reacting sorely to the tongue-lashing they had just received with the rancher's hardly diplomatic accusation that they were all likely to abandon him.

Had Guisewell been capable of self-analysis he might

have found that the morbid twist in his personality dated from the loss of his young bride, though he'd had his share of tough determination and a measure of ruthlessness before that date. A man had to be so equipped to achieve real success in this raw, arid and dangerous country at that time.

In those days he had not been entirely without a sense of justice and fair play. When he created Blue Mesa, his conduct was reasonably straight-dealing and the town's first settlers had little to complain about.

Ultimately, after the loss of his wife and the hardening of his belief that the world was against him, his perspective swerved; he became the man who now rode a dark trail, a grasping, intolerant and deeply suspicious victim of a torturing obsession. At rock bottom he was prone to certain fears that he could not recognize in himself.

As he and his riders left the water hole with all the speed they could muster, the four pursuers waited on the darkened minor trail for a short space in case what had sounded like the beginnings of the Guisewell party's departure was merely a ruse.

Continued silence from the water hole prompted them to approach the erstwhile ambush base. There, stumbling among half-seen rocks and tall saguaro cactus, they found the natural pool, well replenished by the recent rain, and their horses were allowed to drink.

They were now on the trail to Crouching Lion, knowing that Guisewell's riders could not be far ahead.

'I reckon we'll catch up with them easily in daylight,' Young said. 'That's if you boys are not so weary and so wet that you're thinking of throwing your hands in. I wouldn't blame you. After all, you're businessmen, not fighting men.'

'What? Who says we can't fight?' snorted Harry Cornford. 'Heck, I fought with Sherman's Union men in the big war and Karl there was with Carl Schurz's Germans, also fighting for the Union. And Sam Willows, well, he was a blamed Southern rebel, fighting with Mosby's raiders but we forgive him. We belong to the new America now and fight side by side.'

'Well you sure have some impressive military credentials,' Young answered with a laugh.

'Yes, and we just don't like Guisewell. The thought that he's running around with a couple of packs of dynamite is plumb frightening. We're staying hard on his tail.'

As the first glimpse of silver dawn began to streak the sky the four watered their horses, rested for only a brief while, then mounted up and headed in the direction of Crouching Lion.

Hardly half an hour's ride ahead of them the Guisewell riders jogged onward, most of them not in the best of spirits. They were still wet from the drenching rain, and incidents on the trail, such as the halt to block the minor trail by hauling rocks to form a barrier, the desertion of Hartman and Potter and the ineffective exchange of shots in the darkness at the water hole had done nothing to strengthen their wavering confidence in Guisewell.

The rancher's earlier demeanour of conquering general was now replaced by a mood of surly brooding. He rode hunched forward, his mind surging darkly as he was tortured by his obsessive, impulsive nature.

He now had a mere nine men to back him; he had no idea that further treason was being plotted among the knot of horsemen behind him.

Red Musson, a blocky, sandy-haired itinerant of the

owlhoot trail, who had taken refuge at the W Bar G with a string of reward posters in his back trail, was scowling over Walt Guisewell's recent outburst.

The rancher had revealed his secret thoughts about his motley bunch of tough hands, At rock bottom, he saw them all as potential cowards. Musson took grave exception to that evaluation. He decided Guisewell was not worth risking his neck for.

He cautiously slackened the pace of his horse until he was riding at the rear of the mounted bunch, where the two last men were Herb Tolliver and Buck Gage, fellow gun-heavy saddle tramps who were also wanted in places outside New Mexico. He paced his animal alongside them.

'I'm getting the hell out of this fix,' he said in a near whisper.

'You don't mean you're quitting?' gasped Tolliver.

'Sure,' Musson replied. 'I'm quitting. And I'm doing it right now, before full sunup. I'm sick of Guisewell. You heard his opinion of us – he figures we're all ready to quit. Well, I'm damned sure he's not worth backing up. Just remember what he said about the gallows at the end of the trail. Well, I was in on bushwhacking all three of those jokers at Crouching Lion. So were you, Tolliver and you, Gage. If Young gets his way, all of us could finish up hanging.' He spat into the dust and added heatedly, 'Into the bargain, I'm plumb weary of this chasing around on Guisewell's say-so. And for a long time I've been sick of Hazen's big mouth and the way he bulldogs us all.'

Herb Tolliver shifted uncomfortably in his saddle, frowned, felt his neck and gulped. 'You got a point there, Red. I don't like the way this damned chase is going all wrong and I have a healthy respect for my own neck.'

Buck Gage was more circumspect. 'If we turn back, we could run into Young and his bunch. They can't be too far behind.'

'So, we'll ride with shooting irons ready in case we do meet them before we take to the open country. And I'm not fazed by that tied-down holster,' Musson went on scornfully. 'You won't find me running scared of Young.'

'Forster reckoned he's hell on wheels with his trigger finger,' said Tolliver. 'And I'm worried by what he said when he showed up at the W Bar G – all that stuff about hitting us with the law. Maybe he's already organized the law outside of Blue Mesa, ready to come in against us. I don't want to end up throttled by a necktie of hangman's rope.'

'Aw, he was probably exaggerating,' said Musson. 'Just the same, I'm cutting loose. I don't want the US law poking into my past. There are things best kept quiet.' He jerked his hand to a point on the trail far ahead.

'See that bend up yonder? As soon as Guisewell and the rest of the bunch ahead of us go round it, I'm turning my cayuse and heading back down the trail fast, whether you two are with me or not.'

'I'm with you,' declared Herb Tolliver without hesitation.

The spectre of the hangman's rope worked a rapid conversion in Buck Gage. 'Well, so am I. Guisewell can go ahead with his lunacy without me,' he declared.

As the riders neared the bend in the trail the trio at the rear slowly slackened speed until a gap widened between them and the men ahead. Then, as the leaders turned the bend and were briefly out of sight, Musson, Tolliver and Gage quickly swivelled their mounts around and spurred them to ride back along the trail.

Dawn was widening now. The three runaways peered intently at each side of the trail, lined mostly by sun-split rocks and boulders and clumps of desert greenery. Eventually they would find a spot where they could leave the trail and ride on to the wider landscape beyond, to take their chances on the open desert.

Full, rosy sunlight was flooding the scene when Gage gave a sudden warning.

'Look! Right ahead of us!'

His companions saw distant riders on the trail, growing larger. Musson, Tolliver and Gage hastily slithered their six-guns out of their holsters and rode with them held out of sight below their saddle horns.

The four approaching horsemen speeded their pace and Guisewell's three deserters saw that Young, otherwise the gunslinger Hank Teed, was leading.

The distance between the two groups lessened, soon they were within hailing distance of each other. In a cold, colourless voice Young called out:

'Howdy, boys. Don't think of causing a ruckus or you'll get trouble in spades.'

Musson, Tolliver and Gage, with murderous expressions and drawn guns kept out of sight, knew they were plunging into an inevitable kill-or-be-killed confrontation. There was no way out of this fix but to go through with the action.

Musson swiftly revealed his Colt and swung it towards Young. Attempting bravado but with a quivering voice, he shouted, 'We're calling you!'

Young acted at once. No eye could catch the speed of his gun hand, which was suddenly full of a barking revolver. Musson lurched back in his saddle, stiffened as though to attention, then fell forward over his saddle horn, dead.

Almost in the same moment, it seemed, a second bullet from Young ended the existence of Herb Tolliver, who was about to trigger a shot. His whole body went slack and he slumped over with a surprised gurgle.

Sam Willows, within that same moment, displayed some of the prowess he'd gained riding with the Southerner John S. Mosby's Raiders during the Civil War by almost matching Young with his speed in drawing his six-gun. He dispatched Buck Gage with a single shot before Gage had any opportunity to throw hot lead.

Harry Cornford and Karl Hessel waved stinging gun smoke away from their eyes.

'Doggone it! We two Yankees never got a chance to shoot,' complained Cornford.

Through the clearing haze, Young contemplated the result of the fight. Three corpses were stiffening on horses decked with saddles and leather trappings.

With slow deliberation Young left his saddle and walked towards Musson's animal. With an effort, he lifted Musson's bulky form from the horse and dragged it with trailing heels to the side of the trail, where he laid it down,

'Too bad we'll have to leave these gents as buzzard bait,' he commented as he strode back to the horse and began to strip it of its saddle and leathers. 'But at least, we can leave the horses to go free. They'll likely wander and hook up with desert mustangs.'

Willows, Hessell and Cornford followed his example and three corpses were left at the edge of the trail with three saddles and sets of leather trappings piled beside them.

The men slapped the rumps of the horses and, free of their burdens, they cantered off along the trail with the energy of young colts.

Next, the four victors emptied the revolvers and carbines of the three dead men to replenish their own dwindled stocks of ammunition. The weapons were left with the bodies and the piled gear.

Young and his three companions knew that any valuables on the dead men's bodies and their weapons might fall into the hands of any thief who happened along. But, with a shared, unspoken sense of honour, forged on the battlefield, they felt it was bad enough to have taken the men's lives without robbing their corpses into the bargain.

'Looks like these three had quit Guisewell,' said Young, remounting. 'We reduced the odds by three and we know the rest of the bunch can't be very far ahead. Go cautiously from now on.'

They resumed the trail as the sun grew stronger; even after the rain the air was less humid than before the downpour. Gradually their damp clothing began to dry.

In a short time the surface of the trail also began to dry and was soon producing the familiar sandy New Mexico dust, raised by the horses' hoofs. About half an hour after their restart Young and his party began to pass landmarks that Young recognized as indications that they were nearing Crouching Lion.

Squinting ahead, he spotted still-rising dust, which marked the presence of Guisewell's horsemen not far in front. The four increased their speed as the bobbing forms of the group ahead of them appeared then disappeared round twists in the trail.

When they pounded around the final turn, they found they were at Crouching Lion. The trail narrowed there. On the left hand reared the rocky wall, the tumbled scree and boulders that had given shelter to the W Bar G bushwhackers.

A little further ahead was the slight rise of land leading to the cave, which Walt Guisewell was now in a feverish haste to blast apart with his supply of dynamite.

On the right hand there opened the great chasm with the natural rock sculpture rearing over it and apparently gazing into it with the alertness of the untamed animal it so resembled.

Just as the rancher spurred his horse to put himself well ahead of the rest of his remaining six followers and had his whole attention focused on the cave, one of the men at the rear of the group saw Young and his three companions approaching at speed. He gave a squawk of alarm.

The men nearest to him turned their heads, saw Young and his three companions in close pursuit. Some instinctively drew their hand weapons. Guisewell, aware of this disturbance at the rear of the party, swung his horse about and charged back through the group of his half-dozen horsemen.

His face was a mask of determined vengefulness and his eyes glittered malignantly. He saw that the pursuers, obviously spurred by the inevitability of a clash on this narrow battleground, were coming on at a headlong pace, clearly looking for trouble.

With speedy action he dropped his right hand to his holster. It swooped upwards, gripping his revolver. Young and his party, now with drawn weapons, ducked low on the backs of their bucking mounts as the rancher's pistol exploded.

The shot went hopelessly off target, sending a bullet screeching over the ducking heads of Young and his companions. For, at the very moment Guisewell pulled the trigger his horse shuddered and fiddle-footed to hold its balance, because the trail began to shake violently.

Abruptly. both groups of riders were forced to struggle to stay in their saddles as their animals lurched from one side to the other, while the rumbling and shaking of the earth beneath their hoofs grew ever more disruptive in its intensity.

Soon it seemed that the whole world had taken a shivering fit, that even the solid rock wall to one side of the trail might split and crumble.

Then, from the opposite side of the trail, a vast wave of water surged up from the chasm of the Crouching Lion with tremendous force. It brimmed over the edge of the great cleft in the earth, then became an almost monumental tidal wave, pounding both sets of mounted men, threatening to sweep the horses off their feet and their riders from their saddles.

Young was overwhelmed by confused thoughts as he tried to control his frightened mount, which was floundering in the swirling water.

At first he thought that this was a delayed aftermath of the storm that had broken the long spell of heat. Perhaps the water was making its appearance by way of some underground system of channels and caves, possibly linked back to the distant Guadalupe range where the rainstorm had originated.

Then it occurred to him that a corner of the curtain between his own time and that of the old Apache legends had been lifted: the parched land was being refreshed by the blessing of water by courtesy of 'medicine' worked by the Indians' unseen spirits.

CHAPTER SIXTEEN

THE DELUGE

Walt Guisewell, panting, spitting out water and trying to curse at the same time, clung to his horse with his arms around its neck. The animal was up to its belly in water which was surging around mounts and men with a force that suggested that it had a sentient hatred of living creatures.

Guisewell's chief concern was for the dynamite-packed panniers slung in front of his saddle. He was within yards of the cave in the rock wall which, with the incriminating carcasses of the horses it contained, was the whole reason for his desperate flight from Blue Mesa.

He was insanely determined to plant his dynamite charges in the cave and blow it and the evidence within it to smithereens.

This almost unbelievable freak of nature was quite literally swamping his plans. He, his men, their pursuers and the horses of both parties were fighting the imminent danger of drowning in the powerful and unending deluge gushing from the chasm.

The narrow trail was now almost a river in which men and animals wheeled and splashed while the air echoed with harsh human yells and curses and the panicky whinnying of horses. And still, the water gushed around them.

Young tried to both control his horse, floundering in the midst of the water perilously close to the lip of the chasm, and keep his seat in the saddle. Several men from both sides had been unhorsed and were swimming in deepening water.

A sudden eddy swirled past him, seemingly heading back to the chasm like a tidal wave and sweeping past his mount. In it a white, fear-stricken face appeared and Young recognized it as that of the man who had carried news of his arrival in town to the marshal of Blue Mesa. It was the face of the Guisewell hand, Shorty Dix.

As Dix was carried helplessly past him Young could see his terrified eyes.

'Can't … swim,' Dix gurgled:

Young had hardly a moment to reach down, and grab the collar of Dix's shirt. With every scrap of his energy he hauled him up, hung on to him tightly and struggled to push his horse against the strength of the water. A large boulder close to the edge of the chasm stood islanded, not wholly submerged.

Yanking the hapless Dix towards it on his panting, snorting animal, Young managed to drape the man over the high and dry top of the boulder. Dix clutched the rock and lay there, shuddering, gurgling and looking like a landed fish.

Water was issuing from the chasm with renewed force and, as Young tried to manage his horse, another swirling eddy caused his horse to lose its footing. Mount and rider were carried into what had been the centre of the trail but was now a surging river.

They almost collided with another mount and rider. Young saw that the man in the saddle, almost face to face with him and glaring at him with fanatical eyes, was Walt Guisewell.

Almost totally overwhelmed by wild water and struggling with a frightened horse, as Guisewell himself was, Young could do nothing to stop his animal from bumping forcefully into the rancher's floundering mount.

Guisewell, driven by unreasoning hatred, abandoned his own struggles and, risking the possibility of lurching from his constantly shifting saddle he lunged out at Young with a balled fist. Young, trying desperately to control his mount with the rein, was struck a powerful blow on the temple which momentarily rendered him almost blind with dizziness.

Guisewell, leering savagely, managed to follow the blow with a second powerful thump to Young' jaw.

Young, already half-stunned, reeled to one side, seeing stars, almost losing consciousness and nearly pitching into the water. He clutched his rein while the world grew dim around him and his horse, like those bucking and snorting in panic around it, tried to throw its rider. Young's senses reeled and he felt he was being overwhelmed by blackness.

His body slackened; he almost slumped out of the saddle and into the water. Young had a sense of oncoming blackness that threatened to engulf him in the turmoil of the world around him.

Striving to bring his vision back to reality, he realized that someone was clutching him and shoving him back to a sitting position. He willed himself to keep hold of his consciousness, shook his head and opened his eyes.

He found that the veteran Apache, the guardian of the sacred site of the Crouching Lion, was beside his horse, up to his chest in the turbulent flood but managing to keep a firm enough grip on his leg to push him up and secure him in a riding position.

It seemed he had exercised that mysterious Apache trick of simply appearing out of nowhere. For a man no longer young, he had remarkable strength and energy and the swirling water appeared to mean nothing to him. He kept pushing Young until he was upright in his saddle.

Skinny and frail-looking as he was, the Indian gave the impression of some creature arisen out of the water, wholly accustomed to its swirling and whirling and fully able to withstand its force.

More in command of his senses now, Young grabbed at his rein and tried to bring his disoriented horse under control. He croaked a word of thanks to the Apache, but when he turned to look at him he found that he was no longer there.

The watcher over the sacred place seemed to have disappeared back among those few larger boulders along the fringe of the chasm that had not been entirely submerged.

Again, Young wondered if he was experiencing manifestations of enchantment.

Guisewell and his horse had been whirled away from him by the force of the water. Now Young saw that his three companions, along with Guisewell's riders, were trying to reach the banks of loose boulders under the rock wall on the further side of the flooded trail, which had not been engulfed by the water.

Some had already managed to climb up to this dry haven, which shelved upwards from the trail.

A sodden, near-exhausted group of Guisewell's riders were already sprawled about on the rocks, recovering their breath in company with the shivering horses they had managed to haul out of the flood. Cornford and Hessell were in the act of heaving their own animals from the water and on to the rocks.

Then, a little distance away, Young spotted Sam Willows also dragging his bewildered animal from the water. At least for the time being his three companions were safe.

Then Young saw that Guisewell had somehow managed to overcome the power of the swirling water and force his mount towards the upward-slanting tract of dry land that gave access to the cave containing the incriminating animal carcasses. As if urged by demons, he struggled onward, spurring his horse mercilessly to force it through the water.

He was plainly intent on reaching the cave at all costs, meaning to blast it to high heaven with the dynamite in his panniers. Young whirled his horse around and spurred it to labour along in the rancher's wake.

The going was not easy but Guisewell reached the dry rise of earth and, managing to stay mounted, he made a strenuous effort to urge his horse up it towards the great dark mouth of the cave, which had several medium-sized boulders scattered around it.

Young persisted determinedly in pursuing Guisewell. He scanned the tumble of rocks that lay under the rock wall some distance from the cave and saw that those who had reached the dry rocks were assembling themselves into two groups. There were five surviving followers of

Guisewell; the sixth, Shorty Dix, was still sprawled, panting and half-drowned over the rock that protruded from the water.

He had been gratified to see that all three of his companions were safely out of the water, but now he realized that they were less active than their erstwhile opponents, who had gathered themselves into a bedraggled group and were stumbling along the rocks, heading for the cave. Guisewell, now no longer mounted, was now only yards away from it.

The brutish, red-moustached Pete Hazen was leading them, attempting to run with a doggedness that indicated his intention to stand by Guisewell. It was as if this remnant of the rancher's followers now had no option but to cluster together in a self-protective body, knowing that Young and his supporting trio were of a tenacious disposition that would not permit them to cease fighting. Willows, Hessel and Cornford were soon similarly stumbling in pursuit of Guisewell's group, while Young gave all his attention and energy to plunging ahead and driving his mount towards the dry portion of land.

The frightened animal seemed to sense the desirability of solid earth beneath its feet and breasted the water, cooperating with its rider's urgings. All too slowly, the distance between Young and the upward-slanting spit of land dwindled.

On the land, close to the cave, stood Guisewell's shuddering horse with the rancher standing beside it, making frenzied efforts to loosen one of the leather panniers from his saddle trappings. His exertions when fighting to extricate himself and his mount from the water were telling on him and he was obviously fumbling the chore.

He eventually shook the pannier free of its fastening and it dropped to the ground. Guisewell moved around the horse to tackle the second pannier just as Young reached the edge of the spit of land.

Panting and still not fully recovered from Guisewell's punishing blows, Young slithered out of the saddle and began to haul his horse out of the water.

A glance out of the corner of his eye gave him a quick, confused vision of his companions and Guisewell's followers clashing on the tumbled rocks running along the margin of the flooded trail. Each side was taking cover behind the larger rocks and the sun put a sheen on drawn weapons.

Then his attention was taken by the sight of the rancher pulling the second pannier free of its fastenings. Gathering all his strength, he began to trudge up the slanting land on weary legs.

Both opposing factions in the hectic events since the chase out of Blue Mesa were suffering. The night chase; the lack of sleep; the exchanges of gunfire; the clothing sodden by the rainstorm and that near-mystical fulfilment of an old Apache legend, the deluge out of the chasm, were all taking their toll.

Ahead of Young, Guisewell was also toiling up the slope, humping the two panniers towards the opening of the cave. He reached the scattering of boulders near the top of the incline.

He turned his head and saw that Young, having left his mount close to the rancher's horse at the edge of the flood-water, was making as much haste as he could up the slope after him.

Guisewell put the panniers on the ground and dropped

behind a fair-sized boulder near the cave's entrance. He lay on his back, gulped breath into his panting lungs and shoved the boulder with his feet with all the force he could muster. It loosened and began to roll downward.

It gathered momentum and sped directly downward towards Young. Attempting to throw himself out of its path, Young found his reactions were dulled by weariness. He slipped and sprawled on his stomach, facing the rolling boulder that was now almost upon him.

It hit him as he lay there, holding out his right arm in an instinctive reaction, trying to hold it off the impact. The boulder rolled over his arm and came to a halt on his sprawling body.

Young lay gasping and struggling as he tried to rid himself of the weight of the massive rock. A sharp pain stabbed into his arm, followed by an ominous numbing sensation through the whole limb. He managed one-handedly to ease the boulder off his body.

Now he had a clear vision of Guisewell at the top of the upward slant, close to the opening of the cave. He was lugging the panniers along but, like Young, he was wearied by the ravages of the recent hours of pursuit, gunplay and punishment by the weather. He was making very hard going of his progress.

Looking back, Guisewell saw Young pick himself up and begin to stagger up the slope, renewing his determined chase. Young fought for breath and was acutely aware of the numbness in his right arm which hung at his side; he found he could not move it and had the alarming thought that it had been broken by the impact of the rolling boulder.

Walt Guisewell reached the entrance to the cave. He planted his twin panniers on the ground, established himself behind them and unholstered his Colt. With unmistakable fear in his face, he watched Young approach slowly and wearily.

The truth was that Guisewell was scared of the significance of the tied-down holster worn by Young. It had been so since he first received word that the brother of a man bushwhacked at Crouching Lion had shown up wearing the hallmark of a gunfighter. His fear had been intensified by Slim Forster's vivid tale of the fast gun of the man he had known as Hank Teed, who once settled a saloon gunfight in Wyoming single-handedly.

In front of his range crew, Guisewell had kept up his bluster and his tough talk. With them, it was easy enough to maintain the craggy, whipcord-tough persona he had created for himself as a younger man, who had made his mark on a tract of untamed territory.

His set of henchmen were mostly social outcasts who had lived by the gun through a time now beginning to fade, and who were beholden to Guisewell because he offered refuge and paid big wages. When confronting Young himself when he showed up at the W Bar G headquarters, the rancher maintained his attitude of truculent aggression because he was backed by his hardcase crew. But, deep down, he was badly scared.

For quite some time he felt that he was losing his grip on what he liked to call his kingdom; he had a nagging fear that it was because of advancing age. He had formed something substantial out of this stark land by sheer determination, hard work and a measure of ruthlessness and he dreaded the thought of it slipping from his ageing hands.

Latterly his fears had even caused him to engage in murder to safeguard his holdings.

Guisewell had known for years that there were people in Blue Mesa who resented his dictatorial grasp on the town. Having heard from Young that there were elements in town that might explode into revolt against him, his twisted perspective caused him to see the man with the tied-down holster as an instigator of such trouble.

He had mounted his attack on Blue Mesa as a means of quenching the threat of revolt; linked to it was the gun-trap with which he plotted the death of the disruptive intruder into his kingdom. But Young had blown holes in the plot with his quick-trigger savvy.

Now, tenacious as ever, Young was still coming after him like a cat after a mouse.

Guisewell, with his eyes fixed on the tied-down holster, watched Young making an unsteady approach, knowing nothing of the turmoil in Young's mind. Ever since the experience with the rolling boulder only seconds before, Young had been trying to revive feeling in his numbed right arm. He attempted to make his fingers supple again and speedily responsive to the dictates of his will.

He opened and closed his fingers with difficulty as he trudged up the slope, fearing that his gun arm was severely impaired and that his chances of making a quick draw were remote.

Guisewell was almost paralysed with apprehension as Young approached. Although he held a naked gun, he was convinced that this man with a swift-trigger reputation would send his hand streaking for his holster and it would come up in a flash, with a pistol spitting hot lead.

'Keep back!' he shouted in a panicky, croaking voice. 'Keep back, damn you, or – or – I'll ...'

His eye fell on one of the bulky panniers close to where

he squatted and he swung his drawn Colt over to point directly at it, with its mouth only inches away.

'By thunder, I'll fire directly into this dynamite and blow all of us to the skies!' he bawled in a demented shriek.

More shots sounded from men in the neighbouring string of rocks but the action there registered on Young as an unseen sort of sideshow to the drama in which he was involved. He plodded upward towards the cave, watching Guisewell's face contorted by fear, knowing that he might be physically incapable of drawing the speedy weapon that so scared the rancher.

Quite suddenly Pete Hazen appeared on the scene, having clambered over the boulders and rocks to one side of the cave. There was a splotch of blood on his face from a deep graze sustained in the altercation with the three companions of Bob Young.

Whatever else Hazen was, he was loyal to Walt Guisewell. He had detached himself from the action in progress among the rocks and had arrived to support his boss. His expression showed desperation and his bared teeth reflected the savage anger of a wild beast.

He was in the very action of levelling a Colt revolver at Young.

Young saw that he was face to face with two men with six-shooters at the ready. Both had reason to shoot him on the spot and he might be physically incapable of reacting in kind.

He halted his progression up the slope and made a laboured attempt to grab for his gun. An excruciating stab of pain jarred through every sinew of his arm. It brought an involuntary gasp from him the moment he managed to grasp the butt of his weapon. Yet he had the feeling that he had overcome the injury to his arm.

He had a vision of both Guisewell and Hazen staring as if mesmerized by the speed of his draw. For, although it cost him a jabbing pain in his arm, he cleared leather with all his old skill. Without any hesitation, he fired three calculated shots.

Not at Guisewell or Hazen, but full into one of the panniers of explosives beside Guisewell at the threshold of the cave.

CHAPTER SEVENTEEN

AFTERMATH

Echoes.

Only echoes followed the shots into the dyna-mite-packed pannier. Their echoes were flung back from the rock wall and Guisewell and Hazen, frozen stock still, stared bewilderedly at Young.

Where was the expected devastating, life-destroying explosion that should have blown all human life in the vicinity and the branded carcasses to smithereens, as well as reshaping much of the rocky landscape?

There was a long spell of stunned silence in with the three men faced each other, poised with their fingers on the triggers of their weapons, two of which were trained on Young while the other, that of Young, was levelled at Hazen.

Abruptly, Hazen's expression changed, signalling to Young his intention to shoot.

Young fired. Hazen's hefty body jerked back, then fell

forward, lifeless. In a death spasm he flung his arm upward and fired a bullet, which went whining into the air.

At the cave entrance Guisewell still seemed to be stunned by the failure of the shots fired into the load of dynamite by Young to bring about an explosion. Then, abruptly, the death of his foremen caused him to snap out of his bewilderment. He gave an almost animal-like growl of determination, which was all the warning of his intention to fire that Young needed.

He blasted a shot at the rancher, feeling that his gun hand had recovered its usefulness. There was a squawk from Guisewell and his revolver clattered to the earth.

Guisewell was left clutching his right hand and glowering and cursing at Young.

Young moved towards the cave, keeping his gun trained on Guisewell, who was grasping his gun hand upon which a furrow oozing blood had been inflicted.

'I've no intention of killing you,' stated Young in a loud voice. 'I told you I'd hit you with United States law and that's what I aim to do. Better face the fact that you have hardly a man to back you up and you have nothing left to fight with.'

Guisewell crouched part-way into the cave, nursing his injured hand, looking wearied but not yet wholly beaten. Young gave a harsh laugh.

'You were badly mistaken about the new-fangled dynamite. I guess you figured it was just a matter of setting fuses to the sticks and you'd blow to hell and gone the whole cave and those horse carcasses with the brands that'll cook your goose.'

'Yes, damn you, and I came close to doing it,' snarled Guisewell.

Young shook his head.

'But you didn't. I don't know much about dynamite but I do know the sticks have to be properly primed and capped before they can be exploded. Shooting into a package of sticks can do no harm. Whoever supplied the explosives should have instructed you in their properties.'

Guisewell sprang up in a desperate leap spurred by utter frustration. He tried to grapple with Young with his one good hand. Young planted a hand on his chest and shoved hard, sending him staggering backwards. Guisewell fell on his back on the floor of the cave, all fight knocked out of him.

'Better admit you're licked, Guisewell,' said Young. 'I'll allow you deserve some credit for what you did in this country in your young days, but you turned pretty damned bad with age.'

'This territory calls for tough measures,' grated Guisewell. 'When there's need, a man has to take off the gloves and fight back. Hard!'

'Are you saying there was a need to send your bunch of gun-slicks to lay for my brother Dick because you knew he was investigating the disappearance of the men from the assay agency, whose deaths you organized earlier? Why did you want to be rid of them?'

'To protect what I'd built up and all I'd struggled and risked my life for. The Apaches were still raiding when I built a ranch here. A man could be murdered in his bed and, by God, do you imagine I wanted to see the cattle outfit I created and the town I built and the whole of the kingdom I made destroyed by the big money men from back East?'

'What do you mean?'

'I mean the despoilers of the earth: the companies and corporations who seek copper, gold and silver. I mean those money-grubbers who count profits while others sweat and do the dirty work in the field. And what follows the first inkling of an ore strike? A rush of prospectors, the creation of boom towns of tents and shacks, haunted by gunslingers, mayhem and murder, that's what.'

'What noble scruples from a man who packed his bunk-house with gunslingers and used them to kill three men,' snorted Young sarcastically. 'So you figured the prospecrors would find evidence of ore veins in the Crouching Lion locality and bring in a rush of speculators?'

'I knew they would. I knew it for years. An old prospec-tor, down and out, stopped at my place in the early days. I gave him grub and he said he'd come by way of Crouching Lion. In the chasm he'd seen streaks in the rocks, indicat-ing the presence of ore. He was too darned old and tired to try digging any out for himself and there were too many Apaches around at that time.

'I kept my mouth shut about it for years, but I always dreaded finding that another Leadville or Bisbee or a hell-hole like Tombstone, Arizona, all brawling saloons and houses of ill-repute, had grown almost overnight right on my land.'

Young blew out his cheeks in bewilderment.

'By cracky, you're a puzzle, Guisewell. You spout the morals of a Puritan but when the chips were down, you plunged into several murders. Anyway there's some doubt that the Crouching Lion territory *is* your land.'

'That don't matter a damn,' spat Guisewell. 'It was near enough to my land and any boom town would be a blight. So far as I was concerned the region around Crouching

Lion was part of my kingdom: a place I created when others saw nothing here but wilderness, rocks, rattlers and scorpions. By thunder, I put my brand on this forgotten end of nowhere and I was not prepared to see it blotted out.'

He paused, and for a moment a crestfallen expression fell across his face, making Young find a spark of sympathy for him. Then he added, almost in a whisper:

'And, above all, I buried the girl I loved here. The place is sacred to me.'

The crunch of boots sounded at the cave's entrance and Sam Willows entered. His clothing was still sodden and his face was weary but he was grinning.

'They're licked,' he announced triumphantly. 'The whole kit and caboodle of what was left of Guisewell's crew gave up the fight. We skirmished in and out of the rocks yonder, shooting at each other. Karl's ear was nicked but it's not serious, then Hazen got a furrow cut in his face. He decided to scoot over here, to back up his boss, I guess, but I see you fixed him. The rest just up and quit and, with the flood gone, we hauled that little guy off the rock where you planted him in the flood. He had no fight left in him.'

'How many of the others are left?' asked Young.

'Only four all told. Others just dwindled away in the ruckus, glad to quit Guisewell, I guess.'

'And you say the flood has gone?'

'Sure. Darndest thing I know. It kind of flowed back into the chasm, all natural like. The trail is cleared again but muddy.'

Young shook his head. 'Can you beat it? Looks like that Indian medicine worked for us, even though we got sopping wet. I guess it caused us to stop the chase and have our showdown.'

Sam Willows looked at him blankly, not understanding.

'Harry and Karl are down there with all the horses and what's left of the W Bar G crew, all tied up with their own lariats.' He grinned. 'According to them, none were involved in the bushwhacking and they see no point in defending Guisewell. As cowhands, all still had their ropes with their saddles. They're weary, wet and so badly licked they didn't even object to being trussed up.'

'What kind of marshal do you have in Sandy Crossing? asked Young.

'A good one, Ed Browning. He's a straight shooter and plays everything by the book.'

'Fine. Let's gather everyone together and head for Sandy Crossing.'

They made a curious spectacle when they eventually rode along Sandy Crossing's only street just as the sun began to dip in the afternoon sky: a party of riders, all showing signs of recent soaking by water. Some were trussed up by ropes and there was a bulky corpse lying across the back of a horse.

A curious crowd gathered as the party progressed and walked beside them, calling questions to Willows, Hessel and Cornford, whom they knew as fellow townsmen.

Young rode in the lead, heading for the only place he knew in the town, the office of the newspaper where Mike Fraser and his sister were standing outside, watching the procession.

Young grinned at them and raised his hat to Charlotte Fraser.

'We have a package for the marshal,' he announced.

'It's the darnedest package I ever saw,' declared the

intrigued Mike Fraser. 'His office is just along the street. I'll send word to him.'

'No need, Mike. I saw this bunch come into town, looking like they just came off a shipwreck. What's it all about?' asked the deep voice of a powerfully built man who had shouldered his way through the gathering crowd. 'That's Guisewell from Blue Mesa. Why's he all trussed up?'

'We're handing them over to you for safe keeping, Marshal,' Young told him. 'They need to be held pending federal charges of murder and conspiracy to murder. Guisewell's in it deep. He and some of these others require treatment for minor wounds'.

He nodded to the body of Pete Hazen, lying over the back of the horse.

'The dead man is Guisewell's foreman, Hazen. He was implicated in two bushwhackings at Crouching Lion. It's as well that you see his corpse so you can report on the nature of his death. I shot him and you can be sure it was in self-defence.

'Four of us shot three of Guisewell's men on the far side of Crouching Lion. It was self-defence again. They were out to get us but we got them first. Also, there were some W Bar G men killed in Blue Mesa when Guisewell raided the town. That was self-defence again – by the townsfolk.'

'Hell, that's quite a catalogue, but killings off my jurisdiction are a matter for the federal marshal's office at Las Cruces,' rumbled Marshal Ed Browning. 'I'll telegraph him so he can send his deputies out to investigate. In the meantime, you and your friends come to my office to make statements after we put your prisoners in the cells.'

Charlotte considered the appearance of the group of newcomers.

'It seems you need dry clothing,' she observed with concern. 'I'll see if some can be donated after I bring Doc Swartz for your wounded.'

Before moving off down the street she looked at Young, who was hardly a romantic figure, sagging on his horse and still in a bedraggled state. There was a sparkle in her remarkably blue eyes and she lifted his spirits with a bright smile.

Sam Willows paced his horse to bring himself alongside Young.

'When we get through with our business with the marshal,' he said, 'come over to my house. We'll put you up for the night and I can provide a set of dry clothes.' Smiling, he concluded, 'I'll need your protection because my wife will be sore as all get-out at me for getting involved in such a dangerous ruckus – but I enjoyed every minute of it!'

Charlotte Fraser looked up to him. 'Mr Young, you deserve the thanks of the public,' she said. 'Walt Guisewell had little influence here in Sandy Crossing but he represented something my brother and I campaigned against through our paper: the greed of those who maybe started in a true pioneering spirit but, gathering power, ended by riding over everyone. Such men lead to crooked politics and corruption. We want none of that as this territory aims for statehood.'

Young looked like a bashful youngster.

'I never considered myself a public benefactor, Miss Fraser, I looked for justice for my brother. I was sure he was a victim of foul play.'

With unmistakable admiration in her expression, Charlotte Fraser said, 'Do stop being so formal. My name's Charlotte.'

'And mine's Bob,' he answered huskily.

The party from Blue Mesa adjourned to Marshal Browning's office where the surly Guisewell's injured hand as well as the slight injury to Hessell were treated by Doc Swartz. The rancher and his bound followers were lodged in cells.

The corpse of Pete Hazen was left with the town undertaker pending examination by the coroner and Charlotte returned to the marshal's office with an assortment of dry clothing donated by some not ungenerous townsfolk.

A deputy marshal telegraphed the federal marshal on the need to activate United States law in Blue Mesa, where the earlier phase of Guisewell's raid had left corpses and prisoners. Also the matter of recovering the bodies of Dick Young and the assayers from the deep chasm was hammered out.

That night, in a bedroom in Sam Willows's hospitable home, a bone-weary Bob Young prepared for bed. He had enjoyed a good supper prepared by Willows's wife, a tolerant woman who had worried over her husband's long absence from home, but now saw him as a returned hero.

Young sat on his bed and fell into a reflective reverie.

His turbulent existence had so far left him no time for lady-chasing, but this could be his time to reassemble his life. A start might be made by facing the problem of paying a compliment to a woman no longer young but mature, gracious and gifted with a generous good nature.

His compliment should surely be accompanied by a dainty gift, or perhaps flowers. That, of course, would be merely an opening gambit: a threshold to be crossed into a hoped-for new life. The thought of the step unnerved him, but he steeled himself to take it.

He felt he was changing like the West itself as it took new directions, shedding its image of trail herds, dangerous towns and untamed men only too ready to resort to the gun.

Maybe he was destined for a whole new existence in vistas offering something he had once never even dreamed of: loving companionship.

An existence where there was no need for the swaggering gesture of the tied-down holster.